Pinned

SHARON G. FLAKE

SCHOLASTIC INC.

No part of this publication may be reproduced, stored in a retrieval system, or transmitted in any form or by any means, electronic, mechanical, photocopying, recording, or otherwise, without written permission of the publisher. For information regarding permission, write to Scholastic Inc., Attention: Permissions Department, 557 Broadway, New York, NY 10012.

This book was originally published in hardcover by Scholastic Press in 2012.

ISBN 978-0-545-05733-2

Copyright © 2012 by Sharon G. Flake. All rights reserved. Published by Scholastic Inc. SCHOLASTIC and associated logos are trademarks and/or registered trademarks of Scholastic Inc.

12 11 10 9 8 7 6 5 4 3   15 16 17 18 19/0

Printed in the U.S.A.   40
This edition first printing, July 2014

The text type was set in Palatino Linotype.
Book design by Elizabeth B. Parisi

To Mom, Dad, and Aunt Betty. You are the best storytellers that I know. I love listening to the way you all weave a tale. Sound effects. Vivid details. Unique voices. Your stories are as good as any movie. How blessed I was to be born into such a family!   — SGF

THE MATCH

Here's what I like about wrestling. You work hard and discipline yourself, and you can be somebody in this sport. And it don't matter if you big or small. Fat or skinny. Rocking killer grades or not.

A wrestler and his opponent compete for control in a match. A match got three timed periods and a ref to make sure you both wrestling by the rules.

At the start of the match me and my opponent both in neutral position, facing each other. Ain't neither one of us in control or got no advantage. So right then, it's possible for either one of us to win.

In the circle. On the mat. During the match.

My goal is to score takedowns, escapes, reversals, and near falls. To control my opponent, and then hold their shoulders to the mat for a pin. When I show up at a match, I come to win.

Did I tell you wrestling is a martial art? Well it is. Anyhow sometime people say I talk a lot. See you next period.

CHAPTER 1

Autumn

You ever like a boy your friends thought you shouldn't like? Maybe he short. Or his ears stick out. Or he got a face full of pimples. But you like him anyhow. No matter what they say. That's how I feel about Adonis. My best friend, Peaches, say I barely know him. She right. But I been watching him, the way you watch the clouds sometimes and see stuff in 'em that nobody else notices.

I wait for Adonis every morning. He ride to school on a van with eight other kids. I watch the driver lower the lift. Down come a boy in a wheelchair that got a tray attached to it. His arms is frozen in place. His head wobbles, like there ain't no bones in his neck. I try not to stare at the girl coming off next. But I do anyhow. She walking. But not so good. Two canes and leg braces

3

help her get around, but she always look like she gonna fall down.

I'd be embarrassed to ride in that van. Adonis ain't. You can tell by the way he comes off. Pushing himself. Sitting up straight and tall like he headed to a meeting with the principal or the head of the school board, even.

I wave. He don't pay me no mind. I go up to him, saying hello. "I saw the van coming, so I waited for you."

Looking at the pink feather sticking out my hair, he yawns. I stare up at the sky. When he turn his wheels to try to get away from me, I follow. Smiling. Punching the arms of his chair, he stops. "Quit it, Autumn!"

"I just wanna ask you a question." Inside I'm telling myself to think of something quick and make it good. "Do we got practice Friday?"

Adonis is the team manager. I'm one of the wrestlers. The only girl.

Shaking his head. Talking like he grown, he say, "I've texted everyone. The time has changed, that's it. The date is the same." His hands go on those wheels, and he's moving again. Leaving me.

When his new black leather jacket start falling off the back of his chair, I catch it. Handing it to him, I think of all we got in common. Our Snickers bar candy-brown skin. Wrestling. And my friend Peaches — who he don't like.

I'm standing right in front of him. Smiling. Blocking him.

"Autumn Knight. You agitate me!" His chair is rolling my way, so I move before I get run over. He don't go inside the building, though. He stop to talk to one of the kids from the van, laughing after a while. He is always nice to them. Always tutoring or working with them to get them better at something like chess or Scrabble. He's different with me. Always mad like I did something horrible to him. Liking him is a good thing. I tell Peaches that all the time.

"Autumn." Peaches runs up, hugging me. "A ninety-eight on my human geography test." She holding up her paper for me to see.

I ask about Adonis. "What he get?"

She cutting her eyes at him. "What's he always get? A hundred. Plus the extra-credit points."

Under my breath, I whisper, "One day, he gonna be my boyfriend." I look over at him. "Seriously — he will."

When Peaches smiles, you can see her pink gums and small teeth. They not showing now. 'Cause she ain't smiling. She upset with me, asking why I'm worrying about some boy when I'm behind in school. Reading, especially.

Besides, she say Adonis ain't good enough for me. "He don't treat you right. And he's handicapped. Look. No legs." She grabbing both my arms, turning me in the opposite direction. "Plus he's only nice to *them*." She points to Roberto Martinez sitting in a wheelchair, with the wind mussing up his long, black hair. "And grown-ups." She waving at Mr. Epperson, our math teacher.

She not exactly wrong. Teachers love Adonis. The principal shakes his hand most every time he see him. Adonis will do anything for them and the kids on the van. He always trying to get away from me.

Hugging me, Peaches ask if I'm ready for Miss Baker's test. I make a face. "I don't know. I studied."

She and me like sisters. She come to all my matches. I let her wear my clothes. She help me with homework. I'm teaching her how to cook. We gonna open a restaurant one day. I'll be the chef. She'll run the business. We gonna be rich.

Opening her locker, Peaches brings up Emily. Adonis's girlfriend from last year, eighth grade, at that other school the three of 'em went to. Peaches and Adonis go here now; Beacon Academy. It's remodeled. Got a greenhouse. Solar panels on the roof. A fly caf.

She talk about Emily all the time. How her brother beat Adonis up. When Peaches gets to the part about the pond and how he pushed Adonis in, I look at the books in her locker. Lined up. Alphabetically. *Algebra I. Biology. French III. Human Geography.* She in GAT — the Gifted and Talented program. Taking AP and honors classes. Except in math. She flunked that last year. Me and her in Mr. E.'s class. I'm repeating algebra, too.

"Emily had big ones." Peaches holding her hands out past her chests.

Looking at my chests, I'm wondering if maybe that's why Adonis don't like me. "Pancakes," a girl said about them once. They not that flat. But biscuits ain't much better.

Peaches get to the part about his wheelchair — how they found it four blocks from where Adonis was. I sit cross-legged on the floor, thinking 'bout practice last night. This guy on my team quit 'cause he couldn't get with wrestling no girl, he said. "Even at practice." He not the first boy to quit on me. Won't be the last, either.

Adonis got what he deserved, being tossed in that pond, Peaches say.

Shouldn't nobody be treated like that, I tell her. "Even if he did snitch on his girlfriend's brother."

She pokes me in the side when she see Adonis and Mr. E. up the hall. Talking. Like they do every morning. "He always has to have the highest grades," Peaches say. "And be head of everything. Maybe people get tired of that!"

I tell her, "A person's allowed to be smart, you know."

"He's not smarter! He just didn't have six cousins, their parents, plus their two dumb dogs living with him like I did last year!" She slamming the locker so hard, the other ones shake. Stomping off, she say, "That's why I didn't pass math. There was too much racket going on at my house!"

Walking up the hall, we both keep our opinions to ourselves. Then who do I see? Miss Baker. My reading teacher. Peaches shaking her head when I duck around the corner. Yesterday Miss Baker showed me my file. I'm three years behind in reading.

I'm a great cook and wrestler. Gonna make Adonis a great girlfriend, too. But reading — that's gonna take me down. I try not to think about it. Or read too often. That way I feel better about myself.

CHAPTER 2

ADONIS

W ake up, sleepyhead." Ma nudges me. "You're dreaming again. Yelling at that girl. Just go ahead. Ask for
her phone number. Get it over with."

Droopy eyed and yawning, I watch her twist her
long, thin braids into a tight, neat bun. "What time is it,
please?" I mumble.

"Go back to sleep, honey. I'm headed to the hospital."
Ma is a head nurse at Macy Memorial. She looks at
the watch I bought her last Christmas. "It's not quite
five yet."

She kisses me twice on the forehead, reminding me
that autumn is her favorite time of the year. And a
lovely name for a girl. Before she leaves my room, she
says that I may invite her home or to a movie if I'd like.
Slowly, closing my door, she asks if I'll need a wake-up

call. Pulling the blankets over my head, I shut my eyes, yawning. "No. And I do not like that girl. I hate her."

Before our front door closes, I'm dreaming again. I try to keep Autumn out, but she chases me. I have to run fast to get away.

Autumn is wearing track shoes. She says they are magic, superfast. Now she is ahead of me, staring back at my legs.

"Where your wheels at?" she wants to know.

"I have legs. See." I stop to give her a better look.

"Those are just pretend. I got real ones. Wanna wrestle?"

Poof! My legs disappear along with the track. We are on a mat now, wrestling. The ref counts down, while Autumn's strong legs push me into the mat. Her arms and shoulders lean onto mine, like steel digging into dirt. "A pin," she says, kissing me.

"Time's up. She wins," the ref tells the crowd. Under his breath he asks how I could let a little girl like her whip me. Then he stares down at my missing limbs. "Oh . . . you're handicapped."

Poof! I am sitting in my chair in the middle of the gym, with everyone staring as if they feel sorry for me.

"I don't care if you don't have legs," Autumn says, walking over to me in my dream like she did the first time we met in real life. "I still think you cute." Then she tells the audience that I am going to be her boyfriend even if I don't want to be.

I force myself to wake up, and wonder why I dream about her so often. I despise her. Nothing about her appeals to me. All those muscles. Not to mention her IQ. I'm sure it's exceptionally low.

Turning down my covers, I look at my thighs. In my dream I had legs; they were hairy. And had muscles. My feet were the same size as Kobe's — fourteen. Before I transferred from Randolph Intermediate, I never had such dreams. Or missed having legs. They put me in that pond, and changed me. I went from being the supermature, brilliant young man who happened to be in a chair to the boy in the chair who almost drowned.

Reaching for *A Tale of Two Cities*, I think about Ma. She asks me often what I would like to accomplish at my new school. I'd never tell her. Or anyone. What I want is the recognition and respect that teachers *used* to have for me before I was rescued from the pond. I've no interest in a girl who cannot read.

"Oh God. I forgot." Scrambling for my cell, I send out a text message from Coach, reminding everyone to return their permission slips. Mat practice began a few weeks ago. In November, dual meets and tournaments start. This is my first time as a team manager. I want Coach to value my contribution. And realize that I do everything perfectly.

Of course Autumn texts me back.

I'ma sit next 2 u on the bus.

Ignoring her, I jump into my chair. Unlock my wheels. And take a shower. While warm water rushes over me, I think about her. She did not lose one match last season. Hasn't read a book since then, either, I'd bet.

CHAPTER 3

Autumn

When Miss Baker walk into class smiling — like reading is fun — I pick up my pencil and draw two hearts.

Instead of a test, gonna read a play today, she saying. I don't know what's worse. A test or reading a play. Both are bad. "Open your books." She walk over to me, squeezing my shoulder. "Autumn. Read the part of Kayla."

I tap my pencil on my book. Wondering how many freckles she got.

She winks. "I know you can do it."

I don't like to read. It's boring. I tell Miss Baker this all the time. She say not to give up. She gonna help me read better. That ain't gonna happen. Teachers tried before. I'm still way behind.

My parents moved around a lot. So I went to a bunch of different schools. Sometimes two in one year. You put your head down a lot after a while and don't worry about the new stuff they teaching. 'Cause you might not be there for the test nohow. I missed a lot of stuff, I guess.

My goal is to be the best wrestler ever. Not the best reader. I know it's too late for that.

Miss Baker's picking at her hair. A gray, curly 'fro, short as the hair on my legs. Then she clear her throat. "Autumn."

I kick the chair leg in front of me. "Awright. Give me a minute."

Opening the book slow, I read a little to myself to make sure I won't mess up. There's so many words on this page. I know Miss Baker. If I do good on three lines, she'll push me to read more.

The clock on the wall ticks loud as a bomb ready to explode.

I keep flipping pages. Seeing words I never seen before in my life.

This Kayla's sure got a lot to say. Five lines on the first page. Seven on the next. God, she never shuts up. "How long is all this gonna take?"

Miss Baker tells me to begin reading on page one and a few other students gonna be Kayla along the way.

"I can't read with that clock making noise. You got a watch. Why we need a clock, too?"

Miss Baker start counting.

That's all Jaxxon Teagarden need to hear. He sits up, telling everyone to be quiet. "This is gonna be good."

I start stuttering right off. "May . . . may . . . may . . . maybe . . ." It happens when I read out loud. I get so nervous and worried, the words I'm reading double, triple, even.

The laughing comes next. "She . . . she . . . she . . . can't talk right when she . . . she . . . she . . . re . . . re . . . reads," Patrick O'Malley say, laughing so hard, hiccups happen.

I read just fine inside my head. Maybe it ain't fast, like the teachers want. Maybe it's not good enough to sound out big words. But it's good enough for me. "Don't use your fingers," my mother say at home. "You too old for that." "You don't know that word?" some kid in one of my other classes will say. "My baby sister know that and she was just born." Then I come to this class for slow readers and Miss Baker say that reading out loud helps us enoun-ciate better and lets her see how much we improve. But it just make me feel dumb.

I drop the book on the floor. Then kick it. Miss Baker walks over, rubbing my back. Her brown hands feel soft as baby lotion. "Autumn," she whispers. "You *can* do this, baby."

No, I can't.

Not right now.

Not today.

Not ever, maybe.

So I pick up my pencil and finish drawing hearts.

CHAPTER 4

ADONIS

"Pin him, Autumn. Break his arm if you have to." Patricia, who Autumn calls Peaches, leaps from the bleachers, shouting. "This is your house. Don't let no boy beat you here!"

It is our first match of the season. I am sitting on the front row, keeping score. Autumn is on her hands and knees, underneath Randy, in the referee's position. Pacing the sidelines, Coach warns her to keep her head up. "Escape and begin to gain those points back."

Randy perspires profusely. The back of his singlet is soaked. Wiping his forehead, he ignores the sweat dripping from his nose.

Off the whistle, Autumn kicks sideways, flips over Randy's back, standing to gain control.

Everyone is on their feet. Clapping. Stomping. Patricia screams, "Yes! Don't mess with my girl."

Seconds later, they launch at each other. Hand fighting, they each wrestle for control. Autumn puts him in a headlock. Breaking free, Randy penetrates, lifts, and drops her.

She's strong. Coach says those legs of hers could crush someone. They wrap around Randy like swamp snakes, forcing his body to stay put.

I love wrestling. It's like playing chess with your body. You have to be mentally tough, able to predict your opponent's next move. Lazy thinkers do not stand a chance. That is one reason why Autumn perplexes me.

For a second, it looks as if Randy will get a pin. A few moves later and he's under Autumn again. Trembling, he tries to keep his shoulders up, while her hands and body work to hold them down.

The ref drops to his knees and counts. Coach eyes his stopwatch. She pins him.

Patricia stands and chants, "Whose house? Autumn's house. Whose house . . ."

When Randy shakes Autumn's hand to congratulate her, his grandmother grumbles and packs up her things. "She shouldn't even be out there with them boys," she says. "They let her win, you know. Would hurt her if they used their full strength."

LJ from our team is making his way toward the mat.

"All of those boys on her team help her cheat," Randy's grandmother says, finally moving on.

Wrestling is not like other sports. There's no one to help you win. No one to blame if you lose. She's wrong about Autumn. She accomplished this on her own.

"Night, Adonis." Coach shuts his car door. "I can depend on ya, yeah?"

Autumn scoots over, to be closer to me. I promise not to leave before her parents arrive.

Crossing her legs, Autumn rubs her thighs. I do not answer when she asks if I think a girl's muscles can ever be too large.

It's a clear, crisp night. I can see Mars if I focus.

She brings up the match. How can I not say that she did an excellent job? The problem is, it will only encourage her if I do. But our team won tonight also, not just her.

Autumn asks if I like being a manager. I share the position with someone else. He sanitizes the mats, picks up gear, and videotapes the matches. I tabulate stats, keep score, and help Ma wash and fold the uniforms. "I love being a team manager," I tell Autumn. "It will look good on my college application."

She looks up at the sky. "Ain't it nice out?" She tracks the Big Dipper with her finger. "My mother taught me how to find the little one, too."

I concentrate on ignoring her, looking over at the grove of trees just past the parking lot. Students who want careers in horticulture, and such, grow food near there. They pick and sell pinecones during the holidays; and mulch leaves and sell those as well.

Autumn jumps up. "A shooting star!" Facing in my direction, she says, "I got my wish already."

Her parents' car pulls into the parking lot. Putting her wrestling bag on her shoulder, she steps back into her sneakers. "I could wait —"

"My mother is on her way."

Walking backward, her eyes twinkling, she tells me her wish. "A perfect season. A boyfriend —"

Their car horn blares, covering up her words. Her mother is insistent. "Hurry up, Autumn."

When they speed from the lot, rolling over a car block, sparks fly.

CHAPTER 5

Autumn

*M*om and Dad done gone crazy. They got this idea. Read. For one hour every night. Together, as a family.

Improving my reading gonna be a top priority, Mom say, handing me a book. Even more important than wrestling.

Sitting at the kitchen table, my bare feet up, I'm wondering, *Why?* Why they wanna do this now? After a match — I'm tired. Don't want to read. Do homework. Or nothing.

Mom pull out a copy of the same book she just gave me. The same one my father is carrying into the kitchen. He sits down beside me, staring at the blister on my big toe. "Your mom and I don't read good as we should." He turn to the title page. "But we reading better than we used to." He rubbing the back of his bald head. Smelling his fingers. "We making you a promise. You gonna catch up . . . to where you supposed to be. In reading and everything else."

Mom backs him up. "We promise."

"Miss Baker called y'all?"

They both shaking their heads no.

"Mr. Epperson?" Me and Dad scratch our foreheads at the same time. "The principal?" Coach comes to my head next. But he would never think up something like this.

Mom was separating recyclables when she found some of my papers, she say. Math quizzes. Reading tests. Crumpled up in balls. She called Miss Baker, who reminded her that my midterm grades wasn't good, either. Dad talked to Mr. Epperson. Both teachers say the same thing. I ain't stupid. I need to work harder. But they not sure I want to.

Mom and Dad didn't have time for stuff like this before. They was always too tired when I was little. Now I'm too far behind to catch up. Anyhow, I just wanna do things I'm good at.

They apologizing. It's mostly their fault that I'm behind, they saying. But this the year they gonna turn all that around.

They dropped out in tenth grade, she worked at McDonald's, cooking. Quit there to clean hotels. Soiled sheets and wet towels is heavier than people think, she always say. Dad was a dishwasher. Plus he sold blood so him and Mom could go on nice dates. After I came, they moved to another city. Kept moving. Trying to find good jobs with benefits. And not let the landlords know they couldn't pay.

Last year, they got their GEDs. It took 'em two years going to school at night. But soon as they got in the program, we quit moving. Now Dad's got a job threading pipes. Mom's working the register at Kohl's. Right before school started, they told me things was gonna be different. Now I see. They serious.

Mom lays her hand over mine. "You gonna read good enough to get into college." She been believing that since she met Peaches's mother over the summer.

I don't wanna go to college. I wanna be a chef. Run my own restaurant. We got the name: Pinned. Peaches drew the symbol. It's a peach with a diamond safety pin stuck in it. She made us up a saying, too. Pinned: Food so delectable, it sticks to your soul.

Opening her book, giving me more bad news, Mom say I'm off the team if my reading don't improve. "By report-card time."

Jumping outta my seat. My voice louder than a siren. I'm telling them they wrong. "September . . . y'all shoulda said something back then."

My father swears if I yell once more, he gonna let what I'm thinking really be true. Mom saying it didn't come out right. "November's report card comes out soon. You got till your January report card to get yourself together."

"But —"

Dad's opening his book, advising me to do the same. Mumbling, I'm doing what I'm told.

The story is about a boy and his dog. Dad was supposed to read it in seventh grade. He threw it in the trash so he ain't have to. It was too hard for him back then.

Tiny words. Old, yellow pages. That's what I'm seeing. One page even falls out when I touch it.

He went to three different libraries, he say, in three different parts of town to get the books. Mom reads the title. I go to the fridge for grape juice. "Can we do this later?" I take a shot glass full at first. Then I fill up a juice glass. My insides still shaking.

"Autumn." Mom sits a bag of peanuts in front of Dad. "You paying attention?"

I sit down. Reaching for peanuts. Drinking more juice.

Dad goes first. He been thinking about this book since middle school, he say, letting out a big breath. Mom squeezing his hand. Then she give a cheer, like he about to step on the mat or a football field to wrestle or tackle somebody.

When I hear him read, I hear myself. Skipping words. Stopping in the middle of a sentence like a car at a red light. Looking ahead to see what's coming. A big word? One with too many syllables? Words that ain't pronounced the way they spelled?

He smashing a peanut with his fist saying he gotta stop in a minute 'cause he hungry and dinner ain't for a while. His book closes. He walks over to the sink, asking Mom if she want to read.

"He wasn't the kind of boy to get into trouble. It's just . . . trouble always seemed to find him. Serundididy." She put the book to her nose like she need glasses. "That how you say that?"

Dad's looking over her shoulder. "Sirin . . . searin . . ."

I try to sound out the word for them. Miss Baker say that's what good readers do. "Sirin . . ." I pause. "Dip . . ."

"Diddy." Mom smiles. "Sirindiddity . . . tity . . ."

She pointing to another word. "What's that?" Sliding her fingernail underneath it, she spells out loud. *S-P-U-M-E*. We don't know what it means, how to exactly say it.

"*Firstly?*" Dad asks if we ever heard of that word. It's on page twenty-two.

I find another one. "*H-A-R-A-N-G-U-E*," That makes me think of lemon meringue pie.

Dumping more peanuts on the table, Mom ask Dad if he sure this a seventh-grade book. Dad smashes peanuts with his fist, leaving brown skins on the table.

When my turn come to read, I excuse myself. On the toilet. Watching wallpaper birds fly across the ceiling, I wonder what they trying to do to me. Then Mom comes knocking. Dad and her been thinking. Maybe this ain't the right book. Too many big words makes it so you don't know what you reading, she thinks. "He going to the library next week or maybe the week after. Who knows . . . for another one."

I knew it. They don't like reading, neither. I'll get to stay on the team. Finish the season in March.

I'm celebrating, when that word pops in my head. *Firstly.* Don't know why. Maybe 'cause it's got the word *first* stuck inside it. I like being first. Number one. Winning.

CHAPTER 6

ADONIS

From the moment I was born, Ma told me I was brilliant, handsome, and strong.

She named me after Adonis, a Greek god. Stephen was to be my name. But when the doctor delivered me, I hadn't any knees, calves, or feet. Birth defects still happen.

"A boy without legs needs a strong name to stand on." Ma said it right in the delivery room. Then she changed my name. When I was young, I would pretend that I ruled the world: All the presidents reported to me. You do not need legs to dream big. You need to be determined; convinced that it is within you to accomplish great things.

I shave in the mornings, so I get to look at myself a lot. My ears are a bit lopsided. That is my only imperfection.

Muscled arms. Wavy brown hair. Eyes so big and black, they glow. They all add up to me. Perfect.

When I get to the breakfast table, Ma says how handsome I am. She picked out my hunter-green sweater. I chose the jeans. Looking good is a top priority of mine. I try never to give people a reason to doubt my integrity.

I butter her wheat toast while she pours oatmeal into our bowls. Drinking from the orange juice carton, I remind her that I am going to the movies on Saturday with a girl.

She smirks. "Autumn, right?"

Since last week I have been telling her about Raven. I met her at our last wrestling match. She introduced herself to me. I'd never noticed her before then. We have honors biology together.

Raven is short. I like tall, statuesque girls. Her hair is short as well. Long hair is prettier. But she is intelligent. A gifted and talented student. Attractive, too. "Her name is Raven, Ma. She's French and African American. Remember?"

Sitting her chair closer to mine, Ma passes me the sugar. "When you dream about her, then I'll know you like her."

It's unfair. I've talked in my sleep since I was very young. Ma gets to hear what I think. When I was in fourth grade, they bullied me. Students at my school called me iron legs, no legs, wheelie boy, stumps, Disability Don, and other things I care not to remember. I never told Ma. She listened in on my dreams. She called a meeting with the principal as well as the bullies and their parents. I began to watch wrestling on TV after that. Last summer I learned to box a bit, as well. If I hit you, it will hurt. I am disabled. I am not weak.

"Raven. Does she wrestle?" Ma and I watched WWE every Saturday night for years. She knows a few moves, so she is impressed with Autumn. She has never met her. But a girl wrestler seems cool to Ma. Besides, she doesn't think I pick the best girls. She said Emily would get me into trouble. She did. Emily told her brother that I was the snitch. Before then, she cheated on me. Raven is a good girl. Very quiet. I dislike girls who talk too much. I hate the loud, obnoxious ones, especially Patricia (i.e., Peaches).

Ma sits our dishes in the sink. "When you dream about a girl every night —"

"Not every night," I correct her.

"She has gotten under your skin." Ma read an old newspaper article about Autumn. She is determined to go to one of her matches. "She just seems sweet," Ma whispers.

She splashes her uniform, rinsing out the glasses.

I get a text from Raven.

"See, Ma. She's studying while she's eating breakfast. Autumn, on the other hand, is a bad student."

Ma asks what sort of grades Autumn gets. I earned a C once in third grade and cried. I've only gotten As since. Autumn's parents would probably throw her a party if she came home with a C. "I bet she'll have to repeat ninth grade."

"Well — I do believe in doing well at school." She walks over and kisses me on the forehead. "I also believe that we all have gifts. Things that separate us from the crowd."

I've got tons of gifts. I name a few. Ma laughs. "Humility, however, is not one of your gifts."

That's correct. I know who I am. I know what I am capable of accomplishing. I do not dull my light so other people will feel better about themselves.

CHAPTER 7

Autumn

Sweaty. Stank. Ain't got time to freshen up. Gotta hurry and catch him. Wednesdays he got chess club. He runs it. They had one disabled kid before he took over. Now they got four. Two girls, even.

I take the shortcut 'cross the walkway on the third floor, running into Jaxxon, who shoves me, telling me to watch where I'm going. Miss Baker standing beside him, reminding me to take home my book and do the assignment on page thirty. Then she congratulates me. My picture's in the paper. I had five pins — shutouts — in a row: 5-0 (twice), 8-0 (twice), 7-0. They say I got a good chance of making it to regionals. Qualifying for states.

"Our superstar." Mr. Epperson locking the door to the teachers' lounge across the hall. Holding up his grade book, he say, "C minus. You can do better." When I pass him, he ask me to have Peaches come see him before class starts. Bet it's about her last quiz. She got another C. Cried in front of the whole class.

I rush up the hall. Run down the steps. Catch my breath on the first floor. Chill at the elevator, waiting on him. I'm smiling like I'm getting my picture taken when he roll up. "Hey."

He pushes the elevator button. His fingernails clipped and clean. The watch he never take off needs a new band.

I bring up practice. Hook and rolls, knee bars. And Melvin moving up in weight class. All of us happy, 'cause anybody wrestling 195 gonna wish they wasn't.

I tell Adonis how much I miss him when he not at practice. Pulling up my pant leg, I say for him to look.

He's staring.

"At what, Autumn?"

"Check out my muscles."

I got beautiful legs. Nice muscles. Smooth brown skin. I'm hoping he's noticing — but not the brush burn I got on the mat at practice.

He presses the button again. I'm rehearsing in my head what I came to ask. *Wanna go to the movies this weekend?* No. That's not right. *Adonis, you seen that movie they been advertising? The one where the guy's head gets chopped off. Wanna see it with me?* Crap. That ain't right, either.

"Autumn."

I can't help it. He the smartest, cutest boy ever.

"You're talking to yourself. Muttering." Then he starts talking to the elevator. "I'm in a hurry. Come on." Holding down the button, he looks at the floor instead of me.

I lean against the wall, one foot up, thinking. I love smart boys.

Fixing his blue tie. Tightening the knot. He looking like a teacher. Not no kid. "Quit staring," he say, taking off cuff links, digging his fingers into his chair handles.

I can't ask him. He gonna say no. I bring up something educational, instead. I always get more words from him then. "What do the word *firstly* mean?" I can't get that word out of my head. It's stuck there like a seed in the ground.

He a human dictionary. Giving it to me as a adverb. "*Firstly*. It's another way to say *in the first place*." Then I get a sentence.

I wonder about his brain more than about his legs: how a boy can be so smart, holding things in his head the way sugar holds sweet, making people think they know him when they don't. Just like Peaches. I want my kids to be born that way. Smarter than everyone else.

"On the mat, I got skills. Nobody can touch me. But math, reading, I hate 'em." Mom say I shouldn't talk like that. He probably know anyhow. Everyone do. "It's easy for you and Peaches."

"Nothing . . . is easy. I study."

"I mean —"

He turns so I'm facing his back.

In wrestling you learn to ignore stuff. Like when your opponent uses body language to put you in your place. I'd cry if I paid attention to stuff like that. So I walk around till we face-to-face, in neutral position. Sorta like in wrestling. Then I come out and say it. "School is my worst subject."

Maybe I should quit the team, he saying, and study more. He telling me education ought to be my primary concern. I'm sorry I brought up the subject. No one understands.

Moving closer. My knees touching the edge of his chair. I try to make him see. "When I wrestle . . . I, I feel smart. Like I know the answer to every problem every time."

That's why my parents can't kick me off the team.

He looking up at me. Like he getting what I'm talking about. I tell him a little more, my eyes never letting go of his. "I know what my opponents gonna do 'fore they know what they gonna do. But reading —" I quit talking. And think how when I grow up, it's gonna be different. I'll make my kids read while they little. Young as the babies in that television commercial.

Pushing his sleeves up, he tells me how many books he read over the summer. "Thirty-five. A hundred twenty-five books this year already." He naming titles. "Only one had less than four hundred pages."

I worked out all summer. I read one book the school assigned. Miss Baker say that's why I failed my first test. I wasn't prepared.

The elevator doors slide open.

"I like movies better than books."

He don't move.

I look down the hall, making sure no teachers around. Then follow him on.

His fist slams into the elevator wall. "Stop stalking me!" He puts up one finger. Then two. Then five when he say, "You show up at the van. Now you're at the elevator. Last week you were waiting for me after a morning meeting with Mr. Epperson. Plus you came to my AP psychology class. You forgot something, you told the teacher."

It sound wrong when you hear it out loud.

If he had legs, they would be walking away from me right now. "I do not like aggressive girls." Cuff links fall off his lap, onto the floor — rolling into corners like dice.

Bending down, picking them up, I'm trying to explain. "I ain't like that. For real. It's just that — what if I texted you? Would that be better?"

"Are you in special ed?"

I know what he mean. What he trying to say. So I stick him as hard as he sticks me. "It wouldn't be so funny if I said something about you and that chair, would it?" I'm sorry right away. 'Cause I ain't like that.

When the elevator doors go to shut, he stops 'em. "I get straight As in this chair. What do you get?"

CHAPTER 8

ADONIS

Ma pulls up to the theatre, and who do I see? Autumn with Patricia. "Oh God. Why are they here?"

Ma looks ahead, her hands gripping the steering wheel. "Well. Have fun." She peers out of the window at Autumn, and smiles at me.

I am on my first date with a regular — an able-bodied person. I hope they do not ruin it.

Raven climbs out of our van. I lock my wheels in place, and ride slowly down to meet her on the pavement. Ma drives away, waving.

"Adonis. What y'all doing here?"

Autumn cheerily walks over to us. Patricia stays behind. Her lips and eyes reveal what she thinks of me. They roll and twist, along with her body when she turns her back toward me. "Autumn, let's go," she grunts.

They dress alike at times. Today they have on burgundy sweaters and black tights with rhinestone buttons at the ankles. A few guys whistle when they pass by Autumn. They throw their eyes at me. Raven moves in closer, like a pup protecting its territory. Her hand extends when she introduces herself to Autumn. I like mature girls.

It doesn't take long for Autumn to annoy me. She traipses along beside us while we head toward the ticket booth.

Patricia avoids looking at me. "Let's go, Autumn. C'mon." Autumn disappears in the crowd ahead of us. Periodically I can see her looking back at me. A guy standing behind her pulls at her curls. She laughs. He squeezes her arm muscles. "Wrestling . . ." I can hear her say that. "Beacon Academy . . ." I do not hear her finish her sentence since Raven is speaking to me. Patricia glares at me while she purchases her ticket.

I ask the cashier for 3-D, balcony tickets. She looks at Raven and winks at me. "Would you like popcorn? A drink?" I ask Raven on our way inside.

She holds out a crisp ten-dollar bill. "I can buy the popcorn."

I've banked 20 percent of my money since I was six years old. "I'll pay for everything." She smiles on her way to the restroom. Moving quickly behind her, Autumn is smiling, too.

Patricia buys their snacks. While she waits, she focuses on the movie posters. I look at my watch, and then back at her. She told them to put me in that pond. I know it.

I try to forget eighth grade, but seeing Patricia always reminds me of it. I had to tell that Anthony stole the midterm. It was only right. She should have been suspended, too. Anthony swore she had a copy.

Five against one was a fair fight to them, I suppose. And to Patricia. When they dumped me from my chair and tried to drown me, I saw her by the trees, spying. She should have gone for help. Or told the principal what she'd seen.

I get a text from Raven and go to order our food, wondering if she and Autumn are in there fighting, or discussing me.

"Next. Whatcha want?" a cashier says. Looking over my shoulder, I see Autumn rushing toward theatre seven along with Patricia. Whispering.

I do not like carrying trays, so our drinks sit between my hips and my chair. If you stop them from filling the cups to the top, you will not have a problem.

Popcorn, Raisinets, and Goobers sit on my lap as I head for the butter machine, a woman standing close by wants to know if I'll need help. She does not wait for an answer. Her hands grab my tub of popcorn, holding it under the spout. "How much do you need?"

"I'll butter my own food!"

Reaching for the container, I knock over our drinks. Popcorn spills everywhere. Soda and ice splash, soaking my pants, chair, and floor.

Raven walks up to me while the woman is apologizing. Should she call my mom? Do I want to go home and change? She's asking such ridiculous questions.

I dry off some in the men's room. I begin with my watch, wiping it clean, including the face and inside the leather band. On my way out, I still find ice cubes in my chair.

At our seats, Raven asks again, "Are you sure . . . you're okay?" I tell her yes. Only I'm not. Everything bothers me. My chair is damp and sticky. My pants smell of buttered Coke. The regulars — able-bodied people — who saw me in the lobby walk past me, staring. Including the guy who couldn't keep his hands off Autumn.

CHAPTER 9

Autumn

Peaches cracking her knuckles. "Quit that," three of us say. She do it every time we got a test. I'm looking at her legs, smacking her hand. She know what I mean, so her legs quit moving back and forth like church fans. "It'll be easy." I snap my fingers. "Right?"

People think Peaches and me is opposites. When it come to some things, we just the same. Math freaks us out. The reading part is the worst part for me. Tests is her problem. She know the work. But she freeze up, like ponds do 'round here every winter.

Peaches always saying she got a C average in math. It's really a low B. She want to take algebra II over the summer on the Internet. And honors geometry in tenth grade. "So I can't get no Cs or Bs even," she saying. I would die for one of those.

Peaches taught herself to do calligraphy. The pink and purple letter *A*'s she drawing on her notebook look pretty, swirly, curly. Visualize and you get more of what you want. That the kind of thing she say. It ain't working so good for her in math. Or for me with Adonis. This morning at the bus stop, his wheel rolled over my toe.

Mr. Epperson telling us to take out a pencil and eraser. "Sharpen now. Please. No distractions during the test."

He standing over me, loosening his beige tie. It matches his corduroy jacket. His red suspenders look like prison bars trying to keep his stomach from getting away. "You studied, right?" He look like he wants that to really be true.

"I studied." I stare at my desk when I say it.

He clearing his throat.

"I'm not stupid!" I don't mean to yell it. "Most of my homework's turned in and you said I got a C average."

He lowers his voice. "It's more like a D now," he says — bringing up the makeup quiz I forgot to take.

He'll grade my test first if I stick around after class and show me what's not working. "Then I'll see you at tutoring, right?"

How can I come to after-school tutoring plus wrestling when I gotta take the bus home? "Mr. Epperson — I studied. I swear."

I think about Mom and Dad. I lied to them this morning, too. They asked me about that dumb book. I told 'em I would read it by myself. Write them a report, like they asked. The book is under my bed. Or in my locker. Somewhere. But I do got that word, *firstly*, and the definition in a jar in my room. Can't tell nobody. Not even Peaches. You do stuff like that in elementary school — catching lightning bugs in jelly jars, saving rocks in your underwear drawer. But words? Who save those?

Peaches chews on her nails, scratching black polish off. Spitting it out, like it's corn stuck between her teeth. "You know you gonna pass," I say, after he leave. I start to talk about Adonis. She say I better not mention his name.

I ask if she coming over this weekend to cook. I already went to the store, got everything we need. I'm trying to make a wedding cake. Six tiers, my own recipe. I bought the bride and groom. They look like me and Adonis. Only he got legs.

"You make me so mad," Peaches say under her breath. "Talking about boys. Him. Studying when you feel like it." Staring at her tattoo — plump peaches with vines twisting through 'em that she snuck and had put on — she tell me she wanna do more than open a restaurant.

I know. Living in France, being a illustrator, marrying a musician is all part of her plan, too. But this weekend we cooking. "So. You coming or what?"

She trying not to smile. "Yeah. When we get our restaurant, I don't want you talking about secret ingredients. I need to know everything that go in everything."

Mr. E. looking at his watch. "This ain't just a test, folks." He walking the aisles. Patting Jaxxon's back. Telling him to sit up. "It's a competition. Remember." He stop in front of me. "Like basketball. Wrestling." He give a thumbs-up to A'Destiny. "That person next to you, don't let 'em beat you."

December, at the sharpener, finishes his words. The ones he say all the time. "Outthink 'em. Outwork 'em. Outperform 'em." She add her own spice to it. "Kill 'em if you need to."

"Ignore that last part." Belching, Mr. E. ask Jaxxon to take off his hat. "Gas." He's on a new diet, he saying. "Lettuce and more lettuce." Patting Jaxxon on the shoulder, he say for him to sleep at home sometimes.

We have to show all our work in Mr. E's class. If you only give the answer, you lose points, he reminds us.

The first two problems; easy. I write out the steps. Put down the answers. Pat myself on the back. The third problem is hard. Confusing. Just to figure out what it say, I gotta read it twice. It's a word problem. Hate those. I skip to the bottom of the page. Sometimes that's what you need to do. Skip around. But I end up back at the beginning. Scratching my head.

Looking around, all I see are heads down. Fingers moving. December smiling. Julie blowing bubble gum. They always get high marks.

Think. Remember. Peaches and me went over this problem last night. I almost raise my hand for help. But nobody else is asking him for nothing. Putting down my pencil, turning off the calculator, I give up.

Thinking about wrestling. The reporter at my match saying how aggressive I am on the mat. I feel better.

"Three minutes, folks."

Peaches kicks my chair leg, pointing for me to get busy.

I'm writing down anything now. *Don't leave blanks. Guess. You might be right.* That's what she told me yesterday.

Mr. E. pulling at his suspenders. "Pencils down."

Peaches pushes buttons on her calculator faster than a cashier on the first day of the month.

Leaving class. Peaches pulls out her algebra book, checking her answers.

Walking behind her, my book half closed so she don't see, I write:

Firstly I am agressive
I am agressive, firstly
I am
Autumn Knight
Math and reading is agressive opponents to me.

CHAPTER 10

ADONIS

Raven sashays into the library. Roberto pokes me. "She's the kind of girl I want." Leaning over the second floor railing, he gawks and waves.

Her hand, like a fan, waves back. Her silver bangles jingle like tiny bells. I am surprised when she smiles my way.

"Let me see your assignment, Roberto."

He never takes his eyes off her. "Please, can't I look for one more minute?"

Roberto is a seventh grader. He has potential, I've decided. I will give him all the help he needs to succeed. But he has to want this for himself. I've told him several times, "To accomplish your goals, you cannot be distracted by the people and things around you."

Raven takes a seat on the purple couch. Chatting with friends, she looks up at me periodically.

I have avoided her, ever since our date two weeks ago. Last night she came to the wrestling room. I did my best to ignore her there as well. I am certain that she thinks I am rude. Or immature. But I sum up people very quickly. Why spend time with those who aren't right for you?

"Let's get started. Roberto. Take out your paper."

The inside of his book bag resembles a Dumpster. Everything is loose. Balled up. Or empty. Like the Skittles and M&M's bags he sits on the table.

"Do you like her legs?" Roberto is in a wheelchair also. A car accident took his legs away in fifth grade.

I sneak a peek at her legs. Although the trees outside have frost on them, Raven's long legs are bare. Roberto licks his lips. "Her blouse . . . is . . . uh . . . tight, huh?" Her top is orange, which is his favorite color, he says. I do not mention that the Skittles on the bag match the color of her top precisely.

"Did you bring markers?" I ask him.

"Markers?"

I always carry a pack with me. A ruler, paper clips, extra pencils — things like that. Roberto takes paper out of his book bag. Then he opens a warm can of cream soda. The signs overhead say we are not permitted to eat or drink in here. He digs his fingers in a bag of corn doodles, offering me a few.

Roberto is like a lot of students, rules do not mean much to him. That is why I like working with younger students. You can influence them in positive ways. I'm warning him, I won't be able to tutor him until he puts his snacks away. I've gotten special permission from Mrs. Carolyn: Instead of volunteering at the library this week, I will work with him on his research paper. But he must follow the rules.

Holding the can up high, soda streaming into his mouth, splashing over his cheeks, he drinks every drop. He stuffs snacks in his mouth. He goes to the trash can, whistling.

Raven walks upstairs, still smiling at me. I try to recall the exact words of the text I sent her the night we left the movies. I think I said, "You're pretty. I'm busy. I will call you if I ever want to go out again."

It isn't easy keeping excellent grades. Besides, I do not like people thinking they need to help me. All during the movie, she asked if I was okay. I had told her. I was fine. On her way from the girls' room the second time, she brought me more damp tissues and wiped down parts of my chair that I wasn't able to reach. I'd never want anyone to do that.

Walking toward the biographies, weighed down with books, she keeps her green eyes on me. Her two girlfriends do the same.

Roberto returns and hands me his assignment. He has only completed one page of a six-page report. It's written in cursive, not on the computer, which his teacher instructed him to use.

Some of his work is written in pencil, smeared. A few paragraphs are done in yellow ink. Words are crossed out. But his spelling is perfect. His grammar, excellent. "This is a draft, right?"

He pulls his paper from my hands, slowly. Blinking. He did not understand the assignment, he points out. He was too afraid to ask his teacher to explain. And he doesn't have a computer at home. I have an old laptop. Ruffling his hair, I say, "Maybe, if we keep working together, I'll pass it along."

"For real, Adonis?"

I talk to him about proper study habits. "This can be an A paper, Roberto," I point out. "Only you've got to promise me one thing."

Jaxxon walks into the library. Girls on the first floor

start to giggle, while they stand up tall and push themselves out.

Roberto says he will promise me anything, if I'll give him the laptop.

I write myself a note, a reminder to bring it in. "Quit waiting until the last minute." I pull out my index cards. "Only people like Autumn do that." He smiles as if I said something positive about her.

"It's wrong," he says.

I stare at his paper. "What's wrong?"

"Your watch. It stopped. It's not four o'clock."

"Let's ... we have to ... I'm here to help you, Roberto."

We work on his thesis statement. Raven and her friends take a seat on the floor between the stacks. Once Jaxxon walks up, they get as loud as the zoo during feedings. After a while, I go over, asking if they could please quiet down. Jaxxon gives me the finger. Raven follows me back to my desk, still smiling.

When she says, "Hello, Adonis," the bangles dance on her arm.

Sitting on our desk, she thanks me. "By being rude to me, you did me a big favor. I always pick the wrong guys." She pinches Roberto's cheek. "And because of what you did: not texting me back, not speaking to me in class for two whole weeks" — she jumps to her feet — "I went out with Michael Jones Kellerman." She came to tell me about that yesterday, she says. "But you were being you. Obnoxious."

Roberto practically stands up. "Eighth-grade Michael?" Like a thirsty dog, he pants. "I, I like Autumn. That wrestling girl. Maybe she'll go out with me." He pushes his hair behind one ear.

Raven turns on her heels, switching. "Jerk," she says, walking over to her friends. "Double jerk," she yells, looking right at me.

Her friends laugh. Jaxxon cackles louder than anyone — which is ridiculous. I am so far ahead of him — of any of them — I might as well be a comet.

Roberto whispers, "Do you think Autumn Knight would date a seventh grader?"

Packing my things, I inform him, "We will need to do this tomorrow, Roberto. When you are less distracted."

CHAPTER 11

Autumn

*P*eaches in front of our door, shivering in a gray tee and her brother's green jogging shorts. She won't come in. She won't go home. The purple hat she knitted make sure snow don't wet up her hair. Flurries shaped like feathers melting on her cheeks, quick as powdered sugar in warm water.

Mom and Dad in the kitchen with that book. It never did get back to the library. Plus I quit reading it again. "Autumn, tell Peaches. You got stuff to do," Mom saying.

Peaches could come in. Go to my room. Get on the computer. Even eat up there. But she stuck on our steps like a gnome, scared. 'Cause her father is home, mad right along with her mom over that C+ she got on her report card in math.

Punishment in my house never last the whole time. At Peaches's house, you may never get off. "I'm doing the best I can." She rubbing her thighs, warming 'em. "I study and study. Don't I?" Her eyes look tired, like sleep never came last night. "My mother . . ." She shaking so hard, I step outside and hold her. "She don't understand . . . pressuring me only makes it worse."

Leaning her head on my shoulder, she asking herself how she missed earning twenty-five dumb points on our test. She woulda gotten a solid B if she did. Not that a B's the best she can do, she saying. "But it woulda encouraged me."

Patting her back, shivering myself, I'm seeing how lucky I am. I did worse. Ds in math, reading, and English. Plus a C– in science. I got As in culinary, art, gym. And a B in history — we watch a lot of films in there. I'm happy, happy. 'Cause I'm still on the team. Peaches got a three-point-eight average. Can't even go to after-school activities now. Even cooking with me is out, her mom say.

Miss Pattie only graduated high school. She got five kids. And a old-man husband. Behind his back, I call him Grandpa. When it's just us girls, Miss Pattie tell us to get a good education so we don't end up married to a old man who squeaks, and work a job we don't like.

She and her husband got plans for Peaches. She getting a scholarship to college, they say. Plus going to grad school for her MBA. Peaches got her own dreams. Too many, I think. But they hers.

Peaches's mother walking up my street. Her streaked hair long and wild. "How'd you do?" she ask, kissing my cheek, putting her coat over Peaches's shoulders.

I do not tell her my grades.

She holding a cup shaped like lips, brown, and saying how me and Peaches gotta do better. "Adonis with no legs be running circles around you two."

I look at Peaches, wishing I could ask her how Miss Pattie know him. She staring up to the sky.

Miss Pattie is petite. Way shorter than Peaches. Four eleven, maybe. She telling me that Cs is the same as Fs in their house. "Can't run your own business with grades like that," she say, sniffing what I got cooking on the stove.

They walk off together. But separate. Miss Pattie moving fast with her motorcycle feet. Peaches slow, not really wanting to catch up.

Mom and Dad, at the table, when I get to the kitchen. While my gumbo cooking, they wait for me to read. Can't go running if I don't. They letting me complain. Get a drink. Add more okra and red pepper to the pot.

But we ain't leaving the kitchen. Or closing the book, they say. Not until I do what I'm supposed to.

I ain't on punishment. I still get till January to improve. But once they saw my first-quarter grades, they started up again. Reading every night is back on the table. They swear this time, they sticking to it.

Mom slides her book in front of me. Sitting between 'em, with my eyes shut, I wait. And wait. Ten minutes. Then another half a hour. Stirring the pot in between. Finally opening the book, I read. Stuttering. "Hen . . . Hen . . . Henry . . . loved dogs." The last time I read out loud to my parents, I was in third grade. By fourth grade, books ain't mean much to me. Or them.

Rubbing the shoulder that got jammed when the guy tried to pin me last night, Mom say, "Keep going."

Daddy's eyes watering. The gumbo is spicy, he say, spooning meat from the pot. Then sitting down, his chair back on two legs, just like me, he say, "This book is overdue."

I'm waiting for them to say I gotta pay the fine.

He pick out sausage stuck between his teeth. "It been eight years, that librarian said, since it was last checked out." His arm go over my shoulder. "Just sitting there waiting for you."

Mom want me to keep reading. "Then you, John." Already he trying to back out. "Calm down. Visualize." Mom using Miss Pattie's words. "Pretend we already good readers."

Pouring gumbo in bowls. Chewing okra like they Pop-Tarts warm out the toaster. I wonder if reading will ever come as easy to me as wrestling or loving Adonis. "The . . . the . . . the . . . plastic cov . . . er . . . ing the win . . . window was . . . transp . . ." I make the *P* sound, "pa, pa," with my lips. Then start the word again. "Trans . . . The plastic covering the window was tramps . . . pa . . . rent."

My mother and me say the word at the same time. "Transparent."

She claps. "That's a big one." My father covers up one part of the word. Laughing, he say, "Hey, look . . . that's us. *Parent*."

I ain't notice it till he pointed it out. When you find little words inside a big word, Miss Baker call 'em presents. Mom and Dad still excited. Staring at that word, they find more. "Rent. An. Ran." Dad jumping out his chair. "You see that. You see that one. Spa!"

I leave 'em in the kitchen, picking over that word like they picking over a turkey neck at Christmas.

Upstairs on the laptop in my room, I text Adonis. We got a match tomorrow. After practice yesterday, I couldn't find my singlet. He supposed to be looking for it.

U find it?
Yes.
U washing it?
Yes.
Thnxs. I worried bout it.
Studying, Autumn. Have to go.
How yr grades? Report card?
Exceptional.
Oh. Nice.
Nice? Great! Bye.
Wait.
Yes, Autumn. Busy.
Nothin. CU morow. Hey. U comin 2 practice during thankgivin break?

Adonis don't answer.

Lying 'cross my bed. Feet dangling over the side. I reach under my bed for my jar. Yelling downstairs, I ask Mom to spell that word. "Tranx . . . paren!"

Give her a few minutes to find it, she saying, asking what I need it for. Then from the bottom of the steps, she read it, spelling loud and slow.

Writing down each letter. Using the peach calligraphy pen Peaches gave me for my birthday, I stare. *"Transparent.* My big word."

CHAPTER 12

ADONIS

Our principal made a special request. Could I please be a tour guide for visiting state officials today? The state invested a lot of money into our school: built a new cafeteria, put in a pool, created culinary and horticultural programs, plus more. Beyond that, we now offer the most AP courses of any school in the district. That is the most impressive thing to me.

I arrive ten minutes early. The secretary offers me something to drink, and says, "They'll be ready for you in a minute."

"Good morning, Adonis." Mr. Epperson walks in, shaking my hand. He is my mentor as well as head of the math department. I tested out of geometry before I arrived here. An accelerated summer course, curiosity, and hard work made that possible. With his permission,

I am taking AP statistics. I am the only ninth grader in the class. I respect him as a teacher. Very non-traditional. He recognizes my need to be intellectually stimulated.

He's quit belching. A new diet pill advertised on television doesn't seem to be helping him much, either. He's gained back the few pounds he lost.

A few minutes later the outer office is brimming with teachers. They are all from Team B. Mrs. Sullivan, the gym teacher, Miss Taliaferro, who teaches French, along with a few others congratulate me once I tell them why I'm here. "If we had a million of you, Adonis, we still wouldn't have enough." Mrs. Davies teaches art. I'm enjoying studying the Renaissance period in her class.

Finally, the principal walks out. He introduces me to our guests, explaining that Patricia Pressley and I will both be guides. I wasn't aware of that.

Patricia prances in. Late, of course. Winded. "Sorry." She shakes their hands, and introduces herself. They compliment her on her professionalism and her suit. It's black. She's carrying a clipboard, with leaflets highlighting our school. She hands them out, then offers one to me. She picked them up at the board of education, she says, reaching for my hand and shaking it.

"I already know Adonis." It's a limp shake, like holding a raw chicken wing in my hand. "He and I are both in the GAT program." She tells them how much she loves our school. "I know I'm going to get into a really good college after graduating from here."

We begin the tour on the third floor. This is an historical building. Paintings have been on the walls since 1945, when the building was constructed. The painter is famous locally, I tell them.

Patricia's words trample over mine. "If you go to the museum downtown, you'll see all of his work." She's giving them a history of our school and tidbits about the painter. I talk about the floor. It's granite, taken from rock quarries in this region.

Walking backward, pointing high and low, using good English as if she speaks it all the time, Patricia impresses them. I can tell. They follow her and listen to every word she says, as if she were a PBS reporter.

I suggest we take the elevator to the second floor, to see a joint project between our English and art classes. Each team had to build a city. One was made of sugar cubes. The other was made of cardboard. "Houses, graveyards, people, stores, alleys — everything was to be included." The idea derives from the novel *A Tale of Two Cities*. "We are reading that in English," I tell them.

They are impressed. Leaving the elevator, Patricia pops her head into Mrs. Kline's art class. She asks if we may quietly show our guests the projects *her* class has worked on. "The best work gets displayed in city hall for a month," we each say at once. We aren't in the classroom very long.

In the hall, she walks faster than is necessary. "We have a lot of really great students here." Report cards were just issued. "I'm a few points from a four-point average," she boasts.

I almost run over Mrs. Gatland's foot. Stepping aside, she suggests that I go a little ahead of her. Patting my shoulder, she asks how I did this semester.

"I have tough classes."

Mr. Summers knows a lot about me. He gives my GPA and names some of the programs and clubs I'm a part of. "Your principal is proud of you. Three AP classes. A four-five average. Amazing."

They each encourage me to let my light shine, and not to be so humble.

Taking the lead, I explain how vital our school was to the city during World War II. Patricia intentionally stops at the trophy case, asking if they would like to hear about our only female wrestler. They are intrigued to also know that Autumn is Patricia's best friend. We waste lots of time, with her ignoring my hints to move on. But what Patricia doesn't tell them is that Autumn recently lost several matches in a row. I thought Autumn would be upset about it. She wasn't. She has been staying later at practice. Skipping lunch to run and lift weights. Extra efforts work for math as well. You'd think she'd know.

After the tour, the principal thanks us. "You are always magnificent, Adonis." Facing Patricia, he says they were especially impressed with her. "Check in with me once in a while. There's plenty of opportunity for good students to shine." He shakes her hand, smiling. He scurries into his office.

With Patricia walking beside me, the hallway feels as small and tight as a box of matches. Near the library, she shows her true colors. She wouldn't have come if she had known I was part of this, she tells me. Now that it's done, she plans to keep it up. "You not the only smart person at this school. There's lots of us." Her face was soft. Full of smiles earlier. She's frowning now, aiming her eyes at me like they are darts.

Walking ahead of me, swinging that clipboard, she says the principal must be seeing the real Adonis. And perhaps that's why he wanted her to be included. She turns around, walking toward me. "Autumn will see the real you, too." When she brings up the pond and how horrible I've been to *her*, I have to speak up.

"Get away from me, Patricia."

Turning around, making my way up the hall, I feel her eyes on me, as I did at the pond when I asked her to please, please get someone to help me. She stood there like those trophies in the case upstairs, staring at me. Still and quiet.

"Adonis!"

I stop. Gripping my watch, I force that day out of my mind.

Her voice echoes up the hall. "I hate you, too."

I yelled for Patricia until I was hoarse that day. Clawing mud. Trying to keep my face above the water. Sliding under, I'd come up coughing. Holding my arm up high, I begged her.

I had never wished for legs. That day, I did. I hate her for that.

CHAPTER 13

Autumn

Read.
Why?

Miss Baker wrote the first word. While she at the door talking to the librarian, Jaxxon sneaking up, writing the next one. Now Miss Baker wanna know why it's important to read. That ain't a good question to ask slow readers. To us there's never a good reason.

She make a deal with us. If we answer the question, we won't get no homework tonight. Of course she only telling part of the truth. We answer that question and she got three more.

When do you read?
Where do you read?
Why do you read?

My answer take care of all three questions. "I never read." Which ain't the truth. My parents getting on my nerves.

A reading teacher don't want to hear that. Even if she know it's true. Crossing the room, sitting on the edge of my desk, she start talking about my athletic ability. Asking me to name some wrestling magazines. I name three. "See. You do read."

If I want to know a wrestling move, I watch a video, I tell her. People jump in on our conversation. Even if you want to make a pizza, you can find someone online showing you how, Ester pointing out. "So why read about it?"

The rest of the period we talk about our reading habits. Here's what we decide. There's, like, only five reasons why a kid would want to read.

1) They got a text;
2) They on a movie star's blog;
3) Eating cereal. Reading the back of the box makes the cereal last longer;
4) Taking a dump or taking a bath is long and boring without a magazine to look at;
5) They got homework. Which is the worse reason of all to read.

She don't like our answers. But she like that we talking about reading.

When class almost over, she say for us to open our books, swearing we got enough time to get some oral reading in. Pointing to the first girl in the first seat on the first row, she say, "Start reading, baby."

I'm hoping she go from person to person just like that. We got eighteen kids here. By the time she get to me, class'll be over.

"Margaret, read next, please."

Margaret is the fourth girl on row one. You could wash, blow-dry, and braid your hair by the time she read a sentence. Only today she read like she really can read, and the five lines Miss Baker give her get finished in no time.

Miss Baker skips around. Going from the second row to the fifth row to the first. Vera Gunter reads, then Kimberlee, Gordon, and Donelle. I watch the clock. Four minutes to go. Sliding down in my seat, I'm praying she don't see me. She hops to row six, pointing to Barbara Bandera.

"When . . . the girl real . . . lized she was tra . . . She tra . . . She . . ."

I try not to listen to people in here reading. Their words be like my CDs with gum stuck to 'em — hard to understand or follow along. I look outside, mostly. At the sky. Clouds. Even the gray ones. They relax me.

"Autumn." Miss Baker standing in front of me. Waiting for me to read.

I keep watching clouds.

CHAPTER 14

ADONIS

Autumn explodes off the whistle. Intimidated, her opponent backs up, and trips over his feet.

The gym isn't packed. But there are loads of people here. Autumn has her own fan club. Ma is among them.

James isn't wrestling. He is stalling. Pacing to the left. Pacing to the right. Ducking.

"She ain't here to box," someone shouts.

"Take him down, Autumn."

"Girl power," a lady with white hair shouts.

James's coach paces the sidelines. He's asking if this is what he plans to do all season. "Run? Play chicken?" he snarls, and then kicks over a chair. "Get your butt moving, boy! Or forfeit."

Red faced and embarrassed, James rushes forward, his arms pulling, twisting, and turning Autumn's neck, arms, and back. With a double-leg tackle, she lands on the floor.

December screeches, "Autumn! Finish him! He your competition!"

It isn't necessary for girls to scream or shout. Or stump the bleachers as if they need heaven to hear what they are up to. December's hands go to her mouth like a megaphone. "A fall. That's what you came for, girl."

James wins the first round with near fall points.

In stance, they begin the second round. They both move forward, and instantly end up down on the mat.

She gets penalized when she is outside the circle. A six-point lead renews James's energy.

He has her in a tight headlock.

Her feet push down on his ankles. Her body turns in toward his, tied up. They wrestle from one end of the circle to the other, until the clock runs out. "She's good," Ma says, videotaping her for the nurses at the hospital. "Oh my God."

I cannot figure out her obsession with this girl.

"Adonis." She looks at my watch. "The band is frayed."

They are about to start.

"We can afford a new one."

"Ma! I'm working!"

Third period. Autumn takes bottom, kneeling on all

fours underneath James, who has a hand on her stomach. One knee to the ground.

The whistle blows. Autumn does a surprise move. I thought she would drive back into him, standing to gain control. Instead her feet kick sideways. She flips over his back. She stands while the crowd roars.

James did not come to lose to a girl. He penetrates, lifts, and drops her.

Autumn scrambles to her knees. James, riding her back, gets flipped. Landing on top of him, face-to-face, she grunts.

Like contortionists, their bodies twist and turn. Arms bend under backs. Elbows hit ribs. Her chin and neck are being pulled so far up, it looks as if her neck might snap. His ankle gets pounded by her left foot.

Deep inside I'd rather not root for Autumn. But she represents our team. Besides, it is difficult not to be amazed by her strength. The power in her legs. The way she strategizes on the mat. Playing chess with her body out there. I've always loved the beauty and messiness of this sport.

With seconds to go, James goes for a fall. Autumn gets him underneath her. Gritting her teeth, she's pressing in on him. Trembling, she holds him to the mat for three seconds. And wins.

CHAPTER 15

Autumn

*S*kipping, I try to keep up with Adonis. We got our first big snow last night. Plus it rained. Now it's icy, too. I got my tongue stuck out. Catching snowflakes.

His wheels crunch the ice and wet his leather gloves. Walking behind him, I see his bumpy ride.

"Wham!"

A ice ball hit the back of my head. Jason and Kelly from the team ready to throw more. Adonis looking over his shoulders. The next three snowballs come for me, too. "Y'all quit it." I get a few off, then running, I catch up to Adonis. Walking backward, I ask, "What you think snow taste like?" Blowing into my hands to keep 'em warm, I smell breakfast. My very own recipe. Cheerios mixed with almonds, dried cherries, chocolate-covered pretzels, and coconut.

I make another snowball. A mini. "Happy first snow day." Holding it up to him, with a broken branch sticking out of it like it's a candle, I blow. She walks by. "Hi, Raven." I speak first so he know I ain't jealous. I ain't seen them together since the movies, but you never know. He could be texting her.

He don't speak to her at all. She don't speak to him. I can't stop smiling.

Asking questions is the only way to find things out. I ask if she still his girlfriend. Or did they break up? What was it about her that he ain't like?

The questions come faster than foot sweeps when I'm wrestling. He want to know why I think this is my business. When we get inside, his wheels squeak on the wet, slippery floor. A girl walking beside me look over, laughing.

I ask him to the movies. Repeating my question to her friend, the girl say, *"Wanna go to the movies with me? How lame."* She a eleventh grader with long, stringy locks past the middle of her back. Enough blue eye shadow to cover the walls.

They looking at my wrestling bag, hung over my shoulder. We got a match today.

"I thought she was gay," one of 'em say. Turning the

corner, they look back at him. "He in a wheelchair — please. It ain't even electric."

My feet are ice, frozen solid in place.

His wheels seem like wings, flying him away from me.

I wanna go after him. Be with him. Tell him that he gonna ride me to the prom in that chair one day. Roll up the aisle and marry me in it, too. But I stay where I am. In the middle of the hall. Letting people push me, bump into me. Wondering why they can't see me. Or him.

"Something wrong, baby?"

"No, Miss Baker. Just thinking."

She put her arm around my shoulders, forcing me to walk with her.

"I was . . . my class is that way?" I point up the hall.

"Tutoring. I was expecting you this morning."

On Monday I promised her I'd come. "I forgot. I swear."

"That's what you said last week, Autumn."

"Aaahh, Miss Baker —"

She stop to congratulate A'Destiny. Working hard to bring up her grades is paying off, she telling her. A'Destiny got a eighty-three average so far this new semester. "And time to bring that up even higher," Miss Baker say, looking my way.

My rain boots make a puddle. Miss Baker make me a promise. She will no longer come to school early just to accommodate me.

It's easy for everybody to talk to me about . . . not passing a test. Not studying. Not being prepared. But the other day in Miss Baker's class, I took a reading test on a book, a book I read by myself. Got a B. Well, a high C. Okay, I mean a regular one. Answered every question, though. I like that author. Her book is like a movie. Every line is a camera pointing to somewhere interesting. I tell Miss Baker this.

Hugs come from her as easy as batter from a bowl. While she rubbing my back, she warning me. "I already called your mother . . . a little while ago, baby." She told her I missed tutoring. And mentioned that right now a D− is the best grade she could give me, "if grades came out next week . . ." Sometimes she will let you do makeup work. I will earn what I earn this semester, she say, pulling me into the library. "Maybe if you fall far enough . . . fast enough" — stopping, her hands go to her lips, like in a prayer — "you'll turn things around."

My parents said something like that this morning 'cause I didn't want to read that book before school. Had a cramp in my leg. And my belly wanted food.

Talking to Mrs. Carolyn, our librarian, Miss Baker complains. Lots of papers to grade. Parents still calling about report cards. Testing coming up in a few months. "It's too much." Then I hear his name. Adonis.

Turning full circle, I see him, taking a book off the shelf. Still in his coat. Ice caked in his wheels. I'm wondering, *Do other girls think he got pretty lips?*

Mrs. Carolyn asking if I know him. She talking about his "voracious" reading habits, his volunteer spirit, why he's one of her favorites.

The more she say about him, the taller he sits. Perfect posture look good on him. Just like the gray button-down shirt he got on today, and that jacket. It's part of a suit, matching his pants.

Miss Baker say she doing everything she can to get our class to value books and reading. Looking at me, she admits, "Sometimes . . . I'm not sure . . . if you all ever will."

Scratching my nose, and the back of my neck, I remember I'm allergic to libraries. I got a note once so I ain't have to come with my class. After that, Mom said get over it. "Or bring Benadryl."

Three students come to the front desk, checking out books. A girl standing outside the library bang on the window with both hands, waving at Mrs. Carolyn, yelling, "I'll be here fourth period. Save me some food." Mrs. Carolyn having a lunch meeting. Her regulars will eat later, she telling us.

Adonis go over to a table with books piled higher than his chair. Miss Baker and Mrs. Carolyn talking. I'm imagining me sitting in his lap, listening to him read. Kissing him after every sentence.

"Would you like to, Autumn?"

"Huh?"

"Volunteer." Miss Baker smiles. "Didn't you hear Mrs. Carolyn, baby? She wants to see my students in here. Giving back."

"Firstly," I say, hoping he hears me, "I do not like libraries."

They correct me, calling it a media center. Scratching my elbow, I listen to Mrs. Carolyn's commercial on libraries. They are fun. You can make friends. Blah, blah, blah, blah, blah.

Adonis is at the dictionary in the middle of the room. It's big, with like a hundred million pages. Someone donated it to the media center, Mrs. Carolyn saying.

I wonder what part of the alphabet he looking at. *A, F, W*? My favorite letter in the whole dictionary is *Q*. My favorite *Q* word is a name; *Quigley.*

When the bell ring, Mrs. Carolyn asks me to think it over.

Volunteering. At the library. Surrounded by books. Hmmm. But he couldn't get away from me in here. One whole period. Me and him. Once a week. Maybe more. "Okay." I ask to work the same hours he do. He come twice a week, she say. Tuesdays and Thursdays, during lunch.

That's what I'll do. Come. To be with him. Adonis. Who I love.

CHAPTER 16

ADONIS

Your period on?" Tyrelle Davis is sitting on the gym floor with his legs open wide. He does not wait for Autumn to respond. He looks at the guys on his team, then hurls more words her way. "I hate that. Wrestling you when you're menstruating —"

He bends forward to touch his toes. "Same thing last time . . . I can always tell." He pinches his nose closed. "You smell."

There are thousands of people at the tournament. Guys. Coaches. Girlfriends. Parents. With thirty-five schools represented. As usual, Autumn is one of the few girl wrestlers. She has been to the restroom three times since we deboarded the bus. It's because of Tyrelle, Coach said. Tyrelle has never won against Autumn.

"But he gets up in her head like termites in wood — chewing away her confidence."

Our team was given specific instructions. Keep him away from her. "Let the match determine the best," Coach has said. "Not the fists."

I cannot tell if she is shaking because she's nervous or because she's angry. "Ignore him, Autumn. Keep walking. The tournament will start soon."

Tyrelle's team is everywhere. Twice as large as ours, they lay on the bleachers: asleep, resting, talking, stretching. They stand near the walls, working knots out of one another's arms and legs, taping torn wrestling shoes, spying on pretty girls.

Running in their red-and-white uniforms, circling the gym with other teams, they chant, "Raiders, go. Raiders, yo."

Tyrelle brings up the size of Autumn's chest. "Bacon bits." His teammates sitting nearby laugh so hard, they tear up some.

Autumn's knee is a rocket aimed at Tyrelle's shoulder blade. She pounds it over and over again.

He falls over onto the floor, laughing hysterically. I saw him wince when she hit him. It hurt. He deserved it.

A girl in this sport can accomplish a lot. But that does not mean every guy likes it. Most guys do not want to lose to a girl. With us it becomes a mental thing: how to win against a girl and not be embarrassed. With girls, it's physical. We are much stronger than they are.

For Autumn to win so often speaks volumes about her determination, strength, and training. If only she were smart.

Leading her by the elbow, I encourage her to go be with our team. I push my wheels and try to make small talk with her.

Tyrelle is an idiot. He throws his knee pad at her. "For extra protection."

Pow. Tyrelle looks at me, surprised.

I detest violence. I dislike Autumn. But bullies — I hate them more than I hate Patricia. I had to punch him. Sometimes fists are required.

Grabbing both my arms, he tries to pull me from my seat. Fists are flying. Autumn and other wrestlers join in, too. Coaches from other teams try to separate us and calm everyone down.

A ref leaving the men's room gets everyone's attention when he issues us a warning. "Go find your teams, or forfeit."

Wrestlers are exceptionally disciplined, single-minded, and focused. None of them would want to come here and go home without challenging their opponent on the mat. Quietly they walk off, sit down, or put headphones on their ears and close their eyes. Tyrelle passes by Autumn and me. "On the mat," he says to her, "I'm going to finish you."

CHAPTER 17

Autumn

Mrs. Carolyn ask to touch my cheek.
"Go ahead." It's bruised. Black and blue.
Purple, too. Tyrelle's foot hit it. "It don't hurt . . .
too much." I stick my book bag under the front desk.
Proud when I say I sent him home in a arm sling. Bet
he was double mad. I took second place at the
tournament.

Her finger slides over my cheekbone. Then it goes up
to her lips. "Shush." Jaxxon at the computer, talking,
one hand is on the keyboard, one arm is around some
girl's shoulders. His lips head for her mouth. Mrs.
Carolyn is asking them to separate.

She never seen me wrestle. She won't, either. She'd
rather read about some things than watch 'em, she telling me. I look around for him. He here. Avoiding me, I

think. When I came in and spoke, he kept his eyes on the book he was looking at. Sailboats racing 'cross the ocean. That's all I could see. He wouldn't say what he was reading. I asked, then went to look for the librarian, itching.

Standing on my tiptoes, I pull up my pant leg. Showing off the scar under my left knee. I'm proud of that, too. Got it at my first match. I lost. It keeps me hungry, though.

Mrs. Carolyn is expecting a class, so she can't show me around. She told Adonis to show me the ropes. It's my first day volunteering. He can't get away from me now.

A gold top. Matching sweater. Purple scarf. Black tights. That's what I'm wearing. Plus heels. Well, boots with heels. After a match, sometimes it's hard walking in 'em. Everything can hurt the next day. Even feet. Fingernails. Sneezing. Switching can hurt, too. I move my hips and butt side to side, slow and hard. When I get to him, I bat my eyes. Not too hard, though. It makes my ears hurt. Bending down, I press my arm next to his. "We match. Both of us got on gold tops."

The girl with Jaxxon opens her mouth when his lips get near hers. My mouth opens a little, too. I swallow, looking down at Adonis.

He hands me papers. "Here's the list." He pulls a book from the shelf. Sits it on a table. "We're weeding today."

"Huh?"

"Getting rid of old books." Mrs. Carolyn will sell some as part of a fund-raiser and give some away, he saying, looking over his shoulder at her. "Many will end up in the trash."

I sit down cross-legged on the floor. Jaxxon hollers across the room. He got a question about math home-work. I ain't know he did stuff like that.

Adonis ask how I'll work from down here. Holding on to both chair handles, pulling myself up, I stop, bend over, face-to-face with him — closer than I ever been. For a second I smell the soap he washed with and see two cavities at the back of his mouth. I thank him for looking out for me on Saturday.

He's whispering. "I know what you're trying to do, Autumn."

I'm still holding on.

"It's ridiculous. You cannot force me to like you." Trying to get away from me, he backs into a cart. Books fall. I almost do, too.

Catching two books on their way down. Picking three off the floor. I sit them down, checking out the titles. *"The Bean Trees,"* I say out loud. The other titles I say in my head. *Two Trains Running. Kindred.* Even one about moving somebody's cheese.

Jaxxon walks by with a book stuffed in his back pocket. His eyes leave my face, taking their time all the way down to my feet, like I'm the Statue of Liberty and he got all day to look around. "Nice . . . shoes." He walks away backward. Yawning.

Adonis watches him, even when Jaxxon's outside the library, tapping the window on his way up the hall.

Mrs. Carolyn comes over, asking if Adonis is being a proper assistant. "Yes. He's very good." I ask about one of the books I picked off the floor. "May I have this?"

My manners are impeccable, she says, reading the title. It's something about how the universe was formed. The book is so old, she laughs, she bets there were only half as many planets discovered when it was written. "Take your time. Read it. Let's talk."

"Let's talk?"

She hands it to me. "I'm a librarian, Autumn. A Spelman girl, by the way. A student says she wants to read a book. I wanna know what she thinks about it."

Adonis turns his head, laughing.

I could kick myself. I came to volunteer. Not do no extra work.

CHAPTER 18

ADONIS

I forgot everything — my chess set, checkers, dominos, sudoku. I left home early with Ma to tutor Mr. Epperson's students. The regulars — the able-bodied people — I do not like them very much. They are lazy, among other things. Mr. Epperson thinks it will be good for me. Who knows why. I'll work with them once a week because I think he's great.

Every Monday I play games with students from the van during lunch. Thankfully, Ma brought my things to me. Now I'm setting up.

"Hey, Adonis. What you doing?"

Autumn walks over to Roberto, giving his cheek a little pinch. "Hi, Roberto."

Roberto shoves his chair into mine, scrapes Tyreanna's

wheels just to be closer to Autumn. "Autumn. I . . . I . . . like your hair."

She bends down to his height, complimenting him on his outfit. There he goes again. Drooling. Seventh graders and their braces. I point to the box on the table. "Roberto, get yourself a tissue." He wipes his mouth with the back of his hand. I ask if he'd like to help me set up. He reminds me that he has another paper due. "Sure, I'll help you," I say after he asks. He mentions the laptop I promised to give him. I always honor my word. He will receive it after I've worked with him a bit longer.

Autumn walks to the other end of the table, showing us how slow she can move. How tight her pants fit at times. Without my permission, she opens the box of checkers. Roberto backs his chair up, practically taking mine along, too. The chess set in my lap topples.

Picking up the pieces, Autumn asks if I would teach her to play someday. "I always did wanna learn." Queens and kings get put on the table. Smiling, she asks, "What's this?"

"A pawn." I've never liked people to do things for me. When I was young, my father would not permit it, either. How can you be independent if everyone is picking up after you? Reaching behind my back, I pull a stick from its sleeve. They've given me special permission to bring it in. It has a claw on the end. I made it a few weeks ago. Lots of little pieces need picking up on Mondays.

"Sit next to me, Autumn. I'll teach you to play." Roberto's wheel rolls over one of my pieces.

Autumn eats with Patricia every day. Now that she is volunteering twice a week, she says Patricia is a little upset. "Sorry. I have to go."

I look back at Patricia's table. Paper and books are spread about. Hard work isn't all you need to succeed.

More students head toward our table. Roberto is still trying to convince Autumn. "I guess if I eat lunch with y'all, it would be okay." She opens her lunch bag and explains to Roberto why she is only having boiled egg whites and skim milk for lunch. Looking at me, she smiles.

I knock over my drink with my elbow. Rushing to the front of the caf for napkins, she hardly speaks to some of the guys on the team who call her name. She comes back, wiping up my mess. I almost tell her that regulars are not wanted at this table, but Raven walks in. No, she rides in on Michael Jones Kellerman's back. He is her horse. She leans left, and he walks in that direction. She leans right, and he gallops into line.

Patting the chair next to him, Roberto begs Autumn to please stay.

There are chess pieces still on the floor and dirty napkins balled up in front of me. I blurt it out. "Get away from our table, Autumn."

A hand on my shoulder silences me.

"Oh, Ma." I'm mortified. I even want my mother to see me at my best.

She is holding a tray. The aide who usually makes our treats is off today. Ma agreed to fill in. We both forgot them. "They were in the trunk. I didn't remember until I was miles away. M&M's cookies and brownies."

Autumn interrupts. "I bake. Lots."

"Autumn Knight. I saw you in the paper." You would think she was a movie star. Ma mentions the Parnelle Classics and how Autumn dominated a second ranked state wrestler there. Then she compliments her on the highlights in her hair. "Fabulous." Ma promises to come to another match sometime soon.

"When you coming? Which day?" Autumn takes the plastic wrap off the food, sitting it on the table. She hands out snacks to the others.

Now Ma will know how I feel. Autumn is pushy.

Autumn brings up her history teacher. He said if someone is serious about visiting you, or taking you out for a meal, they will give you an exact date. "If you don't, you ain't serious. That's what he said." Biting into a brownie, she starts naming some ingredients Ma might want to include next time. "Tastes good though, thanks."

Ma laughs. "He's right. I'll be there tomorrow." She kisses me, squeezes Roberto's shoulder, then says good-bye to everyone else.

I'm upset with the both of them. But here comes Jeff, leaning on crutches, dragging his left leg. "Ha you doin', Adonee?" We bump fists. "Winning daday." He sits beside me. Tyreanna likes him. Holding his hand, she says hello.

"Cheeker! Play cheeker wit me." Jeff would like to play checkers with me.

"No. We played together last time."

He likes to get his way, so he grunts and shakes his head. He'd like in on the game now.

"Play something else, Jeff."

"Ummmmm. Ummmm." He makes a sound like the buzzer you press to enter our school.

"Quit it." I'm getting a headache.

"Brat." Lisa looks back over her shoulder. "Spoiled always want your own way. No!" She moves over one seat.

Tyreanna says he may play with her.

Jeff fools teachers and scares some students with his noises. He can be pushy and likes to have his way. We all know better. Disabled doesn't mean dumb. Sometimes we take advantage of people who think we are broken or weak.

I let Jeff have it. "Shut up. Play with someone else." I turn to Autumn. "Can't you see I'm busy? Leave! You're giving me a headache. I don't like you. Stay away. God. How can you be so stupid?"

Our entire table quits talking. Guys from our team sitting a few tables away do as well. Patricia calls to Autumn, "Don't be over there with him. Told you how he is."

Mr. E. has lunchroom duty. Mrs. Sullivan is with him. They look shocked. Autumn is ruining my reputation.

Roberto asks why I am picking on Autumn. He apologizes for me. Tyreanna says being rude to a girl is unacceptable. She uses my words against me.

Autumn kneels down. She blinks. Then blinks again. I look away. I do not like to see girls cry.

"Adonis — I still like you. Even if you ain't perfect. But can't nobody talk to me like that." Standing up, she lets the rest of the table hear. "Not even you, who I love more . . . than I love Peaches."

TAKEDOWN

I am not in a wrestling match with Autumn, although sometimes I think she might believe that I am. And she will not take me down. I am in control of my destiny. But on the mat — well — she is one of the best wrestlers there is.

Autumn is extremely good at takedowns. From a neutral position, she controls her opponent and takes them down to the mat, to attempt to pin their shoulders for a fall. There are several takedown moves. The high crotch, the ankle pick, the double- and single-leg takedown, among others. If you successfully control your opponents with the move, you will score two points.

Imagine someone holding your left leg while attempting to sweep your right leg from underneath you. Or maybe you are attacking them. Grabbing the back of their neck and their arm. Pulling. While you also kick away their leg. Attacks and counter-attacks. Pushing and pulling. Strategizing. Changing levels and making moves. This is what Autumn Knight does or faces several times a week. Could you? I could. I can do anything.

CHAPTER 19

Autumn

*M*iss Pattie in front our class, wearing high heels and a PTA pin saying she the vice president. In jeans and a white shirt, she dressed almost exactly like Peaches. Mr. E. says he'll speak to her later. "By phone. For privacy reasons." Miss Pattie's feet stay put. She standing by his desk, with her hands holding Peaches's wrist as tight as skin hold on to bone.

Walking back like he got miles to go. Out of breath a little, even. Mr. E. learning to do things Miss Pattie's way.

It's Friday the thirteenth. Not a bad day. But a different kinda one. Adonis is here at the back of the class watching the show. Seeing me but not seeing me. I wonder. Did he hear what I said? That I love him — more than I love my best friend.

Mr. E. standing with his hands in his pockets, slouching. Miss Pattie is doing all the talking. Words are like weeds in her mouth — they keep coming. No matter how many times Mr. E. tries to interrupt.

"So far this semester, Peaches is more than passing." He belches into his fist. "Her mistakes. Little, silly ones. Nerves, I think." His voice getting lower. We get quiet, especially when he asking 'bout Peaches's home life. Do she got a quiet place to study? he want to know. "Time to relax? To just do nothing?"

Miss Pattie's rubbing her pin, saying Peaches's home life is fine. "It's how you presenting the material. If she's making As in every class but yours — something's wrong in here. Not home."

"She —"

She cuts him off. "We thinking college in our house. You ain't helping her to get ready by thinking Cs is okay."

Pulling her hand free, Peaches moves away from Miss Pattie. "Leave."

It's a little word and a big, giant, stone-cold hard word both at the same time. I can spell it. Write it. But it's Peaches's word. Not mine.

Peaches stops and stares at Adonis by the door. Shaking her head, sitting down, she tell her mother to go home, "Please."

Miss Pattie's heels always scrape floors. Or tap 'em like hammers on nails. "Patricia. I —"

Mr. E. wanna start class. He'll speak to her and Peaches later by phone, he saying. Peaches cracking her knuckles, using her calligraphy pen to say what Miss Pattie don't want to hear.

GO. STOP. CRAZY. PAiN. STUPiD. ANNOYiNG. OVERZEaloUS. TiRED. OVERWHELMED.

The more words she writes, the bigger the letters get — like clouds filling up before a storm.

Leaving. Miss Pattie walks over to Adonis, asking about his mom. He's respectful, but the way he keep his wheels turned away from her say maybe he hate Miss Pattie as much as he hate Peaches.

Mr. E. gives one big clap after Miss Pattie leaves. "Okay, people. Let's get busy." At the board, he writes *Adonis Einstein Anderson Miller.*

I never knew his name was so long.

"This young man works with me sometimes. Tutoring. Grading seventh grade papers." Mr. E. smiling like Adonis is his son. "Genius."

Since we started this new chapter, Mr. E. say, it's clear most of us just clueless. "So let's try something new." He asking a boy sitting by the door to close it. For Jaxxon, with his head down, to sit up. "I'm letting the best student I got explain things to you all."

Adonis sitting in the middle of the room, when a screen drops from the ceiling. A timer on the lights dims the room. He connecting his laptop, holding a laser pointer.

Turning to page ninety-seven, I follow along. He read the problem out loud. Then says not to let math put you in no hammerlock.

Carefully, step-by-step, he making the problem more understandable to us. After a while, Jaxxon sitting up. Eyes forward.

In the dark, with my head as high as a peacock's tail, I write myself a new word.

Proud.

CHAPTER 20

ADONIS

It is awkward, uncomfortable, to be in Autumn's company now that I know she is in love with me.

On the mat, she pushes and pulls her way into a win. Never forfeiting even when she is out of her league. She is determined to shove her way into my life. Regardless of what I want.

The library is the only volunteer experience Autumn has ever had. In private, Mrs. Carolyn told me this could be a very good thing. "Maybe Autumn will learn to love books as much as wrestling." She winked. But something in her smile told me she wasn't counting on it.

Mrs. Carolyn's nutmeg-brown shoes have new soles sewn on the bottoms. I notice them while she walks down the library steps. Pointing toward me, she hands

Autumn a stack of envelopes. "He'll fold. You stuff."
Then she goes to meet with Mr. Webb and his class.

Autumn rolls up her long white sleeves, and kicks
off her shoes. "You like the color pink?" She wiggles
her toes. "See that *P*? On my big toenail? Peaches drew
it." She pulls at the pink feather in her hair.

Showing her the letters at the end of the desk, I
explain how I like to have things done. Already I've
placed labels on most of the envelopes. I began this job
the day before yesterday. "All you have to do is stuff
and seal them."

She scratches her cheek. "You like working here?"

I pick up a letter, folding it so the ends meet perfectly. Then folding it once more, I pass it along to her.
Shoving it in the envelope, she bends a corner, ruining
my work. She is full of apologies. Why can't she just do
things correctly?

I fold another letter. Sliding my nail along the edge,
making a sharp, crisp bend, I put it in the envelope
myself. Now something else on her is itching. Her knee.
The back of her neck, too. She slides her chair closer to
mine. "I'm allergic to libraries, I think."

Saying ridiculous things never seems to embarrass
her. I hand her another envelope, holding it out like a
gift, hoping she'll realize how to treat it this time.

The media center is always full. In between folding, I check out books. I teach Autumn how things work, as I go along. Every once in a while I think about what she said. Loving me is ridiculous. She does not know me. I bet she's told Patricia, who told her she could do better. But I am the smartest boy at this school. She cannot do better than me.

I love to see what other students are reading. I can tell by what they check out if they are good students or not. Autumn frowns at some of the titles. *Of Mice and Men. Bridge to Terabithia. I Know Why the Caged Bird Sings. The Coldest Winter Ever.*

Jaxxon Teagarden walks past Autumn, clapping his hands in her face. You must keep an eye on him. He can be so disruptive. Sometimes he is too difficult for his teachers. They send him to the library to get him out of their hair. "You like him?" Autumn wants to know.

"I don't know him," I reply, sighing.

She wants to discuss Mr. Epperson's class. She congratulates me on the great job I did last Friday. I am proud of myself. The other students appreciated me, I believe. A few clapped when I left.

Rushing into the library, Roberto moves in between students like a skier steering clear of trees. Mrs. Carolyn pokes her neck out, turning her head in his direction.

"Slow down, Roberto. Unless you want a speeding ticket."

I have his schedule in my locker. At the circulation desk, I ask why he isn't in Spanish class. "Autumn" is all he says.

She stuffs and talks to him at the same time — not watching how she places the letters into the envelopes. If she bends another one . . .

With both hands, Roberto sets a box on the desk. "Can I teach . . . you how to play, Autumn?" When he smiles, he squints, like she is the sun shining on his face.

Autumn walks around the desk, kneeling in a short purple skirt.

"Is this okay, Autumn? It's all we got at home." Santa Clauses and sleds cover the wrapping paper on the box. From across the room, Mrs. Carolyn asks if he has a hall pass. Autumn opens her gift. A chess set. Roberto paid for it with his own money. It's wooden, very expensive.

I wonder if Autumn sends thank-you notes after she receives gifts. I have one in my backpack for Mrs. Tarnelle. She baked cookies for our Monday group.

Autumn kisses him on his cheek. Roberto presses

his nose to her neck and sniffs, like tulips are planted there. "Do you know you smell good, Autumn?"

"This the first gift a boy ever gave me." She looks at me. "Thank you. I'm gonna remember what you did forever. When I open my restaurant . . ."

He listens while she talks about becoming a chef and owning a restaurant along with Patricia. "I'm gonna bring you in a coupon tomorrow" — she wipes gloss off his face — "for two free eats at Pinned."

Roberto swallows. "Can I come . . . to one of your matches?"

Mrs. Carolyn asks me to escort him to the door.

When I return, Autumn is checking out books on her own for other kids. One girl has a graphic novel. The next one is reading romance. I'd say they were C students. Maybe worse.

"Adonis?"

"Yes?"

Spinning side to side in a wooden chair, Autumn holds up a chess piece. A king. "I like it that you never say *huh* — even though I do. And you never say *yeah*. *Yes* is nice."

What is she talking about?

"You ain't say —"

I let her know that I never say *ain't*.

It's her favorite word, she says, pointing out that I folded one letter crooked. She holds it up. Without my permission, she turns it into a ball and trashes it.

"You want a coupon?" She jumps up running to assist Mrs. Carolyn, who has an armful of books. Returning, she picks up the conversation. "A coupon for my restaurant."

"No, thank you."

For the next few minutes she tells me all about it. That is when I learn that she makes dinners. Sometimes she sells them to teachers. What's my hobby? she wants to know. How can I answer? She is still speaking. "I'm gonna make Roberto a chess set made of cookies," she lets me know.

She talks about chicken potpie. Red velvet cake. Asian almond chicken salad. Which would I like her to make? she would like to know.

I explain that I only like to eat my mother's food. As we pack our things to leave for class, she hums. It's a song I have heard before. I cannot think of the words.

I wish she would quit it. I have a headache. The first I've ever gotten at a library.

CHAPTER 21

Autumn

*T*his our last test 'fore report cards get sent home. Mr. E. telling us again. Look left. Look right. We all say it together. "That's your competition."

"I don't have no competition in here." December shoves A'Destiny for saying that.

I'm staring out the window at the snow. Flurries. I write that word down. How many *R*'s, though? Two *E*'s? I'll put it in my jar. *Another* F *word*, I think. On Thursday I found the word *fickle*. Rhymes with *pickle*. That made it easy to spell. Laughing, I look up at Mr. E.

"Glad you think math is fun." He stop in front of Peaches. "It is . . . fun." He winks. "Easier to do than losing weight." His hands hold on to his belly, giving it a little shake. "I'm thinking . . . maybe . . . surgery."

Stopping in front of Jaxxon, he say, "You like zeroes, I take it, Mr. Teagarden."

Jaxxon taking his hat off. I'm looking at Mr. E.'s stomach. Jaxxon yawns and goes down again. Mr. E. clap his hands like they are cymbals. When he yell at Jaxxon, I'm thinking it's the diet talking. "What do you do at night, Mr. Teagarden? Why . . . is your head always in the snooze position?"

Jaxxon jumps up, mouthing off about working late. "Doing real work. Not teaching . . . talking about eating lettuce all the time!"

Pushing past Mr. E., knocking papers outta his hand, Jaxxon leave, asking what we all looking at.

Mr. E. looks down, like the papers are rocks too heavy for him to carry.

I never seen him embarrassed before. Beating A'Destiny to the front, I pick up all I can. We all do.

Thanking me, handing out papers, Mr. E. ask me how many wins. I thought I'd have a perfect season. But I ain't disappointed. "Eighteen wins. Five loses. One forfeit. I'm doing good and the season just getting going."

At her house, Peaches got a book with the dates, schools, and names of the guys I went up against. She want me to take pictures, since she stuck at home still not able to go to my matches. We working on a scrap-book. Got three already, with our cooking stuff in it.

I ask Mr. E. if we get a chance before final grades go in to earn a little extra credit. The answer is no. Lately I been thinking — there's a special ed boy who ride the bus with me. What if I end up in a class like that? With kids who read like kindergartners.

"Miss Knight. Get busy."

It's hard paying attention to a test when your teacher up front looking worried about something. Surgery. He don't need to do that. Guess everybody fighting something.

In the middle of the test, Peaches's hands open like a book sitting in her lap. Her eyes go up. Down. Up. Down. Spying on Mr. E. His feet stay crossed on top of his desk. Suspenders holding tight.

Miss Pattie didn't like what Peaches did, not coming to talk to her in class the other day. Plus missing out on those extra-credit points on her last two tests. Maybe Peaches figured cheating was easier than studying hard, and getting chewed out anyhow.

I try to catch her eye. To let her know she don't need to do this. I'm checking on Mr. E., too. Wondering. Do he know? He don't got to do it, either, get stapled or cut. Diet day and night. Not for us.

CHAPTER 22

ADONIS

While Autumn saunters into the media center, the Nazis break down Anne's door. Rounding the families all up. Sending them off to concentration camps.

"Adonis. I —"

"Shhh." Making her wait, I read to the bottom of the page. I've read *The Diary of Anne Frank* before. It's one of my favorite books.

"But —"

Autumn gets so close to my face, her pink lips almost touch the corner of my mouth. The feather in her hair tickles me. "Quit that, Autumn." I'm at the front desk. It's slow. I'm reading. But she only cares about what's important to her.

"I brought you something. Be nice." An envelope sits in both her hands. "Open it." She drew the smiley faces on herself, she explains. The envelope is blue. The smiley faces are lime green. The exact same color as her dress.

Thank you for you know what. I appreciate it. I wouldn't have figured her to have nice handwriting. I pull out a movie ticket. There's a smiley face drawn on it, too. The first gift a girl has ever given me.

"I ain't have the money for two tickets. But give your mom one of these, okay?" She reminds me that Ma hasn't made it to another one of her matches yet.

She sits a cupcake in her palm, pointing to the gummy rabbit on top. "I made 'em. They called Red Velveteen Rabbit Surprise Cupcakes. Peaches made up the name." She covers her mouth with her hand. "Don't not eat them because of her, though."

Ma makes red velvet cakes. But these are different. Red cupcakes with buttercream icing, and white-chocolate curls on top. The gummy rabbit, sitting in the middle, holds a toothpick with a tiny piece of paper attached to it, like a flag. "That writing really says something." She picks one up and reads. "You are a winner." She says she made that one up. "Dreams do come true." Patricia came up with that one. Autumn wanted to write things like be my boo or let's go to the movies, but Patricia wouldn't go along. She bites into one. "Look." There's white filling inside and another rabbit.

When Mrs. Carolyn walks up, Autumn asks if I wouldn't mind sharing my cupcakes with her. I haven't accepted them yet. I am a gentleman, so I tell her yes. Otherwise, what would Mrs. Carolyn think of me?

"Have you tasted these, Adonis?" Mrs. Carolyn asks. Her fingertip has icing on it. Licking it off, she apologizes, because a little falls onto my book.

"No, ma'am." I pick up a cupcake, putting it aside for later. Autumn has icing on her nose. Laughing, she tries to lick it off with her tongue.

Miss Baker takes a shortcut through the media center. Mrs. Carolyn offers her a cupcake, asking if she knows how good a cook Autumn is. Autumn takes tiny bites. Her eyes looking at me even when Miss Baker is talking to her. I'd skip to the gas chambers if they weren't here.

Our library feels like the cafeteria sometimes. People talking. Eating. Laughing. If I were a librarian, nothing like this would be allowed.

"Oh my goodness." Miss Baker closes her eyes. Swallowing, she congratulates Autumn on her culinary skills. "I get red velvet cupcakes at the bakery." She eats her cupcake in four big bites. Picking crumbs from the paper, she asks Autumn if she will make two dozen for her daughter's birthday. It's at the end of the month. Autumn's bare arms rub up against me. "I been working at the library 'cause of Adonis. I made these to say thank you. I'm liking it here." She sits on the desk, swinging her legs.

"That is so sweet, Autumn." Mrs. Carolyn looks at me, approving of what she just said.

"Autumn . . . see, libraries can be fun." Miss Baker rubs her back.

When we go upstairs to put sensors on the books, Autumn keeps to herself. She is working, but not talking very much. Then out of the blue she says, "You should tell me something about you. Something nobody else knows."

Answering her would only upset me. I keep working, instead. I pull the plastic strip off the sensor and press it along the spine of the book where no one will notice.

"You know everything about me." She picks fuzz off the brown rug. "I ain't too good of a student. I wrestle, bake." Taking a deep breath, she finishes, "Still hate libraries. Shhh." She smiles. "Wish you could graduate school and never read a book." She gets really quiet. Then she asks if I ever wish I had legs.

"Huh?"

"I was just wondering. I wonder sometimes lots of things." She tilts her head toward the window. The sun finds her face, lighting it. "Like if I didn't have legs, would I still wrestle or if I didn't have arms, would I cook?" She reminds herself to get a book for her dad. "I wonder if I was disabled, would I still be me way deep down inside?"

I'm thinking, watching shadows cover part of the rug and my wheel. "I never wonder anything like that. I never had them. I don't miss them." I pull up the sensor I just put down, ripping the page. "And I'm me no matter what. That's a stupid thought you had."

She sticks her legs out and kicks her feet like she's swimming. "You never miss 'em, ever?" Before I answer she says if she were disabled, she'd miss them. "Like people with no teeth must miss them sometimes."

Regulars are the disabled ones. They don't think logically. I tolerate them. But it's hard. They say whatever comes into their heads. Like her. Never thinking they might be hurting someone else's feelings. I stare at her legs. Muscled. Strong and pretty. "You don't miss what you never had."

Her skirt moves up when she kicks again. Her thighs — I've seen them a zillion times. Today, I don't know, they catch my eyes.

"I'm just saying. I'd miss 'em, I think. But I wouldn't let that stop me or keep me from doing things or make me cry. You know what I mean?"

"I don't want to talk about this. It's dumb." I almost say, *you're dumb.*

She stands up, leaning over me, holding tight to my chair handles. "Do you think I'm perfect?"

She smells . . . like roses. I swallow.

"Or do you think I'm sort of disabled?"

See, this is what I mean. You can't even talk to a girl like her. "You —"

She moves in a little closer. "If I was in special ed, would I be disabled, or is disabled only for people like you, whose bodies don't — ?"

I try to back up. "We're supposed to be . . . working."

She says she likes talking to me. "You make me think about important things." Changing the subject, she asks if I wear shorts in the summer.

My hands go up. I almost shove her. "You are absolutely the rudest girl ever."

I'm backing up. She's walking toward me. "I mean, if I was disabled, I'd just let people ask any question they wanted."

She turns and walks in the opposite direction. Following her, I try to give her a piece of my mind. She's still talking.

"I'd say, just give me all your questions at one time." She kneels down, writing on a tiny piece of paper. "You know why I'd do that? 'Cause people always thinking anyhow. They wonder why I read so bad. I tell 'em before they even ask. Teachers get your last year's grades before you walk in class anyhow. So the first day I just tell 'em we gonna have a hard year." She slaps her hands. "Math don't like me. Reading ain't my friend."

"It's not the same, Autumn."

She turns, looking at me. I think she has on eye shadow. And liner. Navy blue. "I like talking to you. Do you like talking to me?"

It takes me a while to answer. "I don't want to talk about my legs."

Scratching her nose, she says, "We can talk about my legs." She kicks one out. "You like 'em?"

"No . . . I mean —" She gets me all confused. That's why I don't like her.

She looks out the window, up at the sun. Closing her eyes, she says, "I think you like me, Adonis Miller."

I punch my hand over and over. "Where'd you get that?"

"Peaches —"

I warn her. "I hate her. Don't *you* ever mention her name to me again."

Autumn jumps from one subject to another.

"You don't make sense." I said that too loud. "You talk too much." She says everyone says that, even her parents. "And —" *I don't like you, so quit antagonizing me.* I'm all set to say that. But that day in the caf, she was supermad at me. Really hurt. I went too far, saying what I thought.

Finally she says she has to go. She'll see me at practice. Then, while she's passing by me, a note falls in my lap. And she's gone.

After I've finished volunteering, I open it.

Disabled is me not being able to read. And you with out legs. So (u + me) = perfect. Right?

CHAPTER 23

Autumn

M r. Epperson up there winking at me. Asking 'bout my opponent and how well I did against him. Only I ain't sure which one he talking about. The boy I wrestled last night or algebra? Or someone in this class? Then he stick my last test paper in my hand.

Peaches jumping up and down, screaming, after she get her paper. "Nice job. A hundred percent," Mr. E. say, loosening her arms from around his neck. "Autumn. Finish handing these out."

Calling out names, sitting papers on desks or sticking 'em in hands, I get to see how everybody else did.

If grades was trees, mine would be the root. At the bottom, way down low. Nobody did worse on this test than me.

December got a ninety-two. A'Destiny got a seventy-six. When I take my seat, she turn around, asking what I got. I make a D– in the air with my finger. Sitting at his desk, Mr. E. saying maybe now Peaches's mom will get off his case. He smiling. But I know what he mean.

The whole period Peaches leave her A paper sitting out like a prize she won. She and me. We talk about everything. Our periods. Cute teachers we wish we could date. Miss Pattie and the PTA president arguing the other night. But cheating . . . on the test. She ain't mentioned it yet.

Picking up my paper, I shake my head. 'Cause today really sucks. This morning Miss Baker say she calling my mother. And report cards come out soon.

Mr. E. ask to see me when class ends. Jaxxon and a couple of more people get called up, too. He concerned we don't understand the material. If we get any further behind, he afraid we never gonna catch up. The six of us crowd around him, hoping people walking out the room can't hear.

"You six. You're all in competition with one another." He points to us one by one. "For last place."

Markey takes his eyes off the floor. And looks at me.

Mr. E. lets everyone hear what my grade average is so far. I get to hear theirs.

"Is this legal?" Markey wanna know.

Mr. E.'s eyes smile. "Miss Knight. If this were a wrestling match . . . you would win against them. You're an A-plus wrestler. So tell me. How can you be a D student?"

Mr. E. looking at Michelle from Mrs. Carolyn's book club. Her average almost as low as mine. He asking how many books she read this month. "Three." He ask Markey if he belong to any clubs or teams. He don't. "Go to church?" Markey says yes. Mr. E. closing his grade book. "Out there" — he's pointing toward the window — "you all do your best. In here . . . the bottom is good enough for you. I need to know, why?"

Markey's hands, deep in his pockets. He saying he gonna be honest. "I can't do it. I quit trying."

Jaxxon laughs, listening to all of us say the same sorta thing. Mr. E., holding on to his suspenders. He want to know if Jaxxon got something to contribute to the conversation.

We need to get to class, we saying.

He ask Jaxxon to stay. "Tutoring, folks. Tomorrow. Or else."

On the way out, I'm listening to Mr. E. apologizing for yelling at Jaxxon again the other day.

In the hall, running fast as I can, I think about Peaches happy with a A she didn't earn. Taking the steps down to the first floor, I'm trying not to think of nothing to do with school. Got practice later today. Gonna get a A in that.

All summer I did drills. Sprints. Leg lifts. Back hops. Knee ups. Sweating in a hundred-degree heat. Lost two pounds a week sometimes. Quit getting perms. I ain't pass my reading tests when I got back to school. But I passed Coach's test. "Condition. Lift. Run. Wrestle. Strategize." That was *my* summer homework.

CHAPTER 24

ADONIS

It doesn't seem to bother Autumn that puddles are underneath my wheels. She is still kissing me. Her lips are as warm as July at high noon. Firecrackers heat up my body. Her smile fills up the sky.

I sit up, wondering about that dream. Lying back down, I can still hear her say it: "I love you." I reach over to my nightstand, reading her note again. How many times have I read it? Every day. Three times a day, sometimes: *(u + me) = perfect.*

At night in my dreams, it is worse than ever. She won't quit saying it. Or showing up.

Smashing pillows over my head, putting two more between my thighs, I close my eyes. I have been thinking that I might quit the library. Work isn't getting done.

I like everything in order. I want to know what to expect every day. Autumn means that nothing is the way it's supposed to be. Chaos should be her name.

Closing my eyes, I remember her cupcakes. Ma texted her to say they were exceptional. Now a seven-layer coconut cake is sitting on our table. Ma paid Autumn to bake it. I had a slice before I fell asleep. It was the best I've ever tasted.

I can make myself dream whenever I like. Or stop my dreams like they're wheels at a high curb. This time when I hear her laughing, I do not try to run. Watching her sit on my lap again, it occurs to me: I've never had a girl love me before. Even when they've liked me, something felt wrong. Cuddling Autumn, I remember I do not really have any friends. Just people I do things for. Those girls, they wanted things, too. Raven asked if I would tutor her right before the movie lights went down.

Autumn is talking a mile a minute, so I kiss her. When I stand up, she hits the floor. *Girls always want something,* I think. I hold on to my dream, even though Ma is calling, trying to wake me up. And Autumn is back on my lap, asking again if I'd like more of her cupcake kisses.

"Coconut cake for breakfast, Ma?" I take ham from the fridge. Yesterday's dinner, fried up with eggs, is what I'll eat.

Ma does not have a slice of coconut cake on her plate. It's a hunk. "She's just a kid," she says. "How does she bake so well? Like a professional?" Her fork slides slowly into her mouth. Closing her eyes, she sits back, enjoying every bite. She makes me wish I had a slice.

We are going over our schedules. It will be a busy day with wrestling, and her double shift. Lately I've been asleep before she's gotten in. Coach offered me a ride.

I'm not talking much after a while. I am planning out my day in my mind. But Autumn keeps popping up. Ma will say her name or I will remember something she did in the library to upset me. The funny thing is, sometimes when I come off the van, I'm expecting her. When she is late for school or absent, it feels weird. Then she comes, and I am really, really angry that she's there. At the library she pesters me; in the hallway she follows me, I'm telling Ma. She says that I am smart about so many things. However, this time, I'll need more than my brain to figure things out.

CHAPTER 25

Autumn

*S*low, like something deep inside him is broke, my father gets off the couch. Stopping in front of me, lifting my chin up, he make sure we seeing eye to eye.

"Your grades don't surprise us none. But . . . well . . . we not gonna help hold your head underwater no more, and cry about you drowning."

I bring up Friday's match. "Y'all coming? Bancock High is three blocks from here." I'm staring at the floor when I say it.

He look at Mom. She looking at me, holding her hand out for my jacket.

I can't walk. Not one more inch. Six guys came to practice late. Every time one walked in, Coach made us do another lap. Someone mouthed off. That meant extra drills later on. Coach was in a bad mood. "Mom. Can you get me a towel?"

Sitting on the floor, pulling off my sneakers and wet socks, I bring up my ranking. Eighth in the city. Number one girl in the state. I can do better.

"You listening?" Mom's reading off grades. I only did a little bit worse than last quarter. It's hard doing sports and being a good student, I'm saying. She sit on the floor beside me, tucking her skirt between her long legs. "No more wrestling. This season anyhow."

"I got a two-point-zero. They let you wrestle with that."

"You gonna be . . ." She looking down at the rug. "Like me . . ."

He swallows. "And me," he says, sitting beside her.

I stand up over them like the flag outside our school, my arms and hands waving. Pointing at them, I say it's their fault. Moving like trains all the time. Pulling me outta schools. "Kids called me stupid, because of y'all."

"We —" Mom stops herself.

Walking in circles with them in the middle, I tell 'em what I never told nobody. "Wrestling was all I had when y'all ain't care."

Dad's tired eyes following me. His fingers lying over Mom's hand, scratching her nail polish. "We always cared," he whispers.

"Not about reading."

All I had when I went to a new school was wrestling. When teachers gave me Ds and notes for home saying maybe I should be tested for special ed, I had WWE and two old mattresses that moved whenever we did.

In sixth grade, when the moving stopped, I got on the team. Even though I wasn't no A student or grade-level reader, it was me shining for once. Like wrestlers on TV.

Yelling. My voice filling the room like ragweed in spring, I tell 'em, "I ain't quitting!"

Mom tiptoeing into the kitchen. Coach is on speakerphone when she get back.

"Tell 'em, Coach. I gotta wrestle!"

Dad saying he got bad news. Today is my last day on the team. Until maybe next year.

Screaming at the top of my lungs. Turning over the coffee table. Throwing magazines. I threaten 'em. "If you don't let me wrestle —"

Coach tries to look out for me. "Autumn! What's going on over there?"

"Y'all can't stop me!" I push my mother. "Regionals . . . the state championship . . . they starting in a couple of weeks."

Dad steps in front of me. He asks Coach if he seen my grades.

"No. But —"

Mom spits the Ds out like they sour grapes.

Coach wants me to finish the season. They not great grades, but they good enough to keep me on the team, he saying. "Mr. and Mrs. Knight, I'll tutor her myself." He stops and asks his daughter to leave the room. Mom listens while he tells her how hard I've worked. What an asset I am to the team. "She can pull those grades up next semester. Can't ya, Auddy?"

Last year my report card wasn't so good, either. I brought up my grades, some. Mom telling Coach, "Long as she reading below grade level —"

I walk out the room. Slamming the china cabinet door. Banging on the kitchen table. Kicking the pile of clothes Mom ironed and folded. My father asking if I'm crazy, saying I got five minutes to pull myself together.

Homemade pineapple upside-down cake sitting on the table, under glass. I take a slice, biting into it, crying. "Y'all got me eating." Crumbs fall on the floor. "I ain't supposed to . . ." Opening the door, I throw the whole cake into the snow. "We got weigh-ins tomorrow. I can't get fat."

In the living room, I hear Coach asking if there's anything he can say or do to change the situation. "We count on Autumn. She's one of our best." The season's gonna end in about six weeks, he tells 'em. "Maybe . . . after everyone is more calm, ya can discuss things."

My father and mother sorry, they saying, to let down our team. "But we can't keep letting her down." Mom cracking her knuckles. "She ours." She clears her throat. "Who gonna look out for her, if we don't?"

Dad asking Coach if he know how it feel to read poorly.

It takes him a while to answer. "No, sir, Mr. Knight. I've always been pretty good at it."

Dad brings up the jobs he ain't get 'cause he couldn't read the applications. "If I did get the job, I ain't have the best benefits. Couldn't read good enough to choose the right health plan for myself."

Mom's crying. "Me. A grown woman. Asking people at work . . . to read . . . my paycheck."

Coach say he'll leave us to our private time and see me tomorrow to talk.

On my knees, begging, promising anything, I say, "I'll be good . . . I'll study. Every day. All day. Please, Mommy . . . please."

Her and Daddy walk into the kitchen, holding hands, talking 'bout Miss Pattie. They gonna call her in a little while.

CHAPTER 26

ADONIS

Some people wait for things to happen. Leaders make things happen.

I will make that point today when I speak to our entire seventh-grade class. The topic is leadership, one of the core values of our school.

In sixth grade, Beacon Academy students focus on community: what it's like to be part of a group responsible for themselves and others. In seventh grade it's leadership: how to speak up, stand up, and take the lead at school, in the community, and around the world.

Eighth graders focus on excellence. They learn not to take shortcuts, how to be their best, and why it's important to put their full effort behind all of their endeavors.

Upper-level students are expected to incorporate all the values they have learned since first attending the academy.

There are some interesting people sitting on the stage beside me: a law student, the city's police chief, the head of Manor Hospital, two blocks away, as well as the principal and the seventh-grade student-body president.

Walking up to the microphone, the principal asks each of us to stand or wave while he does the introductions. From the rear of the auditorium, a voice says, "Wait. I'm here." The principal explains to the audience that Patricia Pressley will also be speaking.

Patricia is a ham. Walking up the aisle, she bows and blows kisses. She has on another suit, navy blue. The portfolio she carries matches her shoes, also navy. I cannot get away from her.

Each of us quiets down, when the principal tells the audience why we are all here. Patricia sits tall and erect, her legs crossed at the ankles, her hands sitting open in her lap. I wonder about her speech. What she'll talk about.

We each get seven minutes. I began to prepare my speech a month ago. You have to write and rewrite if you want it to be exceptional.

A few of the students who ride the van with me are sitting up front, waving. I take my place beside the podium. The principal politely hands me the microphone while students clap. "Leadership" — I pause before I say another word — "is what you do. Not what you say." I am counting in my head — one, two, three — so I do not rush my words. "I think I was born to be a leader." I talk about Ma, who gave me an ultimatum when I was seven. I did not want to join the scouts, because no one else in my troop was in a chair. She took me to the meeting anyhow. She said I could sit in the back of the room alone, or join in the fun. "She promised to pay me fifty cents for each pin I earned. I've always enjoyed earning money. I earned plenty of it my first year. I never got to spend the money, however."

The teachers have to settle some students down. They are complaining that Ma did not keep her word. After one student shouts, "She lied," a teacher walks over and has a talk with him.

"I could keep the money, Ma said, or donate it to a child who really needed it. *Leaders,* she told me, *think of others, not just themselves.* I cried when I put the money order in an envelope to mail it. I was saving to buy a motorized plane. Now I'm glad I gave it away."

I like the mic and stage. Especially when people applaud.

Patricia forces me aside when she walks up to the podium. "You know you are a leader when . . ." She gives ten ways students may develop their leadership skills. She hasn't found her niche at school, she tells everyone. But at her church, in her community, she does a great deal. "I'm the choir director."

I didn't know that.

"Friday, on bingo night, I call the numbers for seniors. Anyone got forty-eight blue?" she says to make them all laugh.

There is more to Patricia than I knew. On Sundays she oversees the children's room for the two- to four-year-olds at her church. "Leaders is . . . are . . . everywhere," she says, pointing into the crowd. "It's in you to lead. You have to believe that."

She tells them to hold hands with the person on each side of them. "Now pull," she says, swaying. "Like you're holding onto a rope." The principal loves her concept, that leaders pull others along with them. "Helping everybody see," Patricia says, pausing, leaning forward, looking at the crowd, "that they have potential. And are strong and smart in their own way."

The teachers jump up, clapping. The students are on their feet as well. Slowly, Patricia walks over to her seat, looking as if her mind is miles away.

After our presentations are done, I head for class. On the way to the elevator, Patricia passes me. "How can *you* give a speech on leadership?" I ask. "Leaders don't —"

She never looks back, or says a word.

The elevator doors open. Mr. Epperson is on it. Asking how I did on my report card, he shakes my hand. "All As, right?"

"Yes, sir."

He has missed several days of school this week. When I ask about how he feels, he changes the subject. He asks if I will help a few more of his students.

I don't know how I can find the time. He wants me to really consider working with this one girl. "She wrestles."

"No." The word jumps from my mouth. "What's wrong with her, Mr. Epperson? Is it ADD?"

"ADD? Nah. Behind in reading. Much rather be out there shining on the gym floor like a strobe light than taking math, that's for sure. But slow? No." Before he goes into the men's room, he says I would be good for her. "You're very clear when you explain things. Math is your gift. Think about it."

He stops, holding on to the wall. He doubles over.

"Are you okay?"

He's on a vinegar-and-water diet, he tells me. "Just a little light-headed."

I cannot figure him out. He is so intelligent and kind. Who cares if he's fat?

CHAPTER 27

Autumn

*P*eaches never cut class. I didn't, either. Till today.

Sitting at home. Watching TV. I wonder what people thinking about me, the wrestler who can't read.

I know they gonna write about it. Somebody probably texting the newspaper right now. I just want to wrestle. What grades got to do with that?

All season you gotta cut weight, watch your weight. Last night I ate a half gallon of ice cream by myself. Chocolate chip with pistachios. At breakfast, I had a pint more.

Pouring flour in a bowl, soda and salt, too, I stir so hard, my arm hurts. I make my own pancakes. Strawberry, from scratch. I can eat as much as I want now. Can't wrestle. So who cares.

Coach gonna have to tell the team. They'll know I let 'em down. It's not right. I got the grades — my parents are doing this to me.

Running upstairs, I grab those books off their night-stands. And dig out the one under my bed. I take them all outside and throw 'em as far as I can in the snow. Then I change my mind. My parents just gonna dry 'em off, and say we got to get back to reading. After all this time we just on chapter four. "Can't y'all see we can't read," I yell. Walking outside barefooted, I put 'em as deep in the trash as I can.

They never did return those library books. At night sometimes I hear 'em reading out loud to each other. Dad say they never will get through. Mom keeps push-ing. If they could make it through a GED program, she said, "a book shouldn't be too hard."

On the Internet, checking YouTube, I find myself waving, walking onto the mat, making mad moves. For two hours I sit, watching. After a while I'm so upset. Tyrelle's gonna make it to states. "Mean as he is." I can't even finish the season.

I'm ignoring all the texts Peaches sending me. 'Cause it's her mother's fault. I know it. Miss Pattie want everybody's children to be like hers — sad.

I throw the plate at the wall. "I ain't going to college. I can't read — shoot!"

Flopping down on my bed, kicking at the window, I scream, "When's it gonna stop snowing? I'm tired of it! I hate it!"

On my computer, I hear people cheering.

CHAPTER 28

ADONIS

Autumn walks into the library, sitting down beside me. She does not say hello. She does not ask what we will be working on today. Her lips are as still as my wheels.

Mrs. Carolyn offers her grape juice from last night's author's talk. "Everything okay?" she inquires.

Autumn does not look up. Or respond. Mrs. Carolyn doesn't press her. She whisks by, asking the assistant principal if he has a minute.

It is nuts in here. A lot is happening. Roberto and his class are researching upstairs. He hasn't seen Autumn yet. Miss Bullard and her class are on the first floor, using the computer lab. Two teachers in the back room are picking up class sets of books. *To Kill a Mockingbird*, *Middle Passage*, even Shakespeare. I bundled the sets.

Then there's everyone else: Jaxxon, cheerleaders meeting about a fund-raiser, maintenance men measuring shelves and checking the ceiling for water damage. It's difficult to concentrate. But not because of them. It's her. Autumn. I've never seen her sad before.

It makes me uncomfortable, the way she sits here, staring at her fingers. For ten minutes and sixteen seconds, that's all she's done.

Two girls walk up to our circulation desk to return books. "Are you Autumn Knight?" You can always tell when they're sixth graders.

The Asian girl elbows her friend. "It's her." Her cheeks turn pink. "I come to see you wrestle."

Her friend takes out a spiral notebook. Ripping papers, she asks if Autumn would mind giving her an autograph. "Me, too." The girl with the blond ponytail covers her lips with her hands when she speaks. "My brother goes to Willard High. He wrestles heavyweight."

Giggling, they slide the paper toward her.

Autumn ignores it.

Crossing her legs and waiting, Maggie, the blonde, cocks her lips to the side.

Maryanne hunches her shoulders. "Well . . . bye."

They're walking arm in arm, then speeding up once they pass the dictionary and running out of the door.

Roberto is chasing someone downstairs. Autumn looks up for the first time. "I don't wanna see him." She jumps off the seat, and stays in the back room until his class leaves.

When the period is over, Autumn and I go up the hall. I have AP statistics. She's going to Mr. Epperson's class. Usually I go to the men's room, that way I'm done with her until practice. Today I head straight for the elevator.

She leans against the wall. I press the button. When the doors open, I hurry on to get away from her. She'll cry soon. Anyone can see that. Knowing Autumn, her tears will drown us all. She can't do anything right. Messes. Problems. That is all she knows. I like intelligent girls — girls with class, who study hard. They know what *firstly* means.

She stops the elevator doors from closing. Crying, she gets on.

I don't have tissues. I don't have time because my class begins in a few minutes and I still have to go to the end of the hall on the third floor, where the door to room 301 always sticks. And I do not have legs . . .

for her to sit on. She sits on my lap anyhow. No girl has ever done that. Has ever wanted to. "Autumn . . . I . . . I . . ."

When her head lies on my shoulder, her curls brush my bottom lip. "I can't wrestle. They kicked me off the team." Tears drip onto my new shirt, steam pressed exactly the way I wanted this morning.

"My grades . . . reading . . ."

In my dreams, I kissed her. Only this is real life. While the elevator rides up and down again, I sit holding her. Thinking.

CHAPTER 29

Autumn

I been wanting to sit on his lap since I met him. Been wanting to know how it feel cuddling up close to him. Don't remember nothing about it now. Hopped off his lap, got off the elevator soon as the doors opened.

"Autumn!" He called me. He wanted me to come back on the elevator. That never happened before. I ain't even turn around. I couldn't.

Running. Up the hall. Over the bridge. Past sixth graders lined up to go on a field trip. Past the horticultural club carrying snake plants into the main office. I'm thinking about the newspaper article. It didn't say why I wasn't wrestling, just that academics was involved.

Running. Down steps. Past lockers and the pool. Past varsity boys, who call my name and try to pump fists. I stop, out of breath. Hands shaking, I pull open the door to the wrestling room.

Lying on the mat, pressing my nose into the thick, blue rubber, I smell yesterday. Practice. Underarms and scalps that needed washing. "Autumn."

I freeze.

The door closes.

It ain't the end of the world, he saying. I got the brains and the mind to do in school what I do in here. "Strategize. Achieve ya goals."

We always teasing Coach about his feet. A big man like him walking on his toes like a dancer. Can't hear him coming half the time.

Squatting beside me, out of breath, he reading off my stats for the season. Then he say, "Tournament Saturday. Ya coming?"

"Huh?"

"Ta support your teammates?"

"No."

My teammates supported me 100 percent when I was wrestling, he saying. "They still do." Then he bring up the guys on the team who lose week after week and don't quit, on themselves or the team. "Wrestling can teach ya something when you losing, too, Auddy."

Can't come to no matches, sitting and watching everybody else winning, guys from other schools asking me why I ain't in there. What I'm gonna say? I can't read? I'm stupid? Grown-ups don't know nothing.

Coach's feet walking across the mat. Light from the hallway shows through the door he holding open. "What if I tutored ya, Auddy? On my own time?"

"No!"

Before he leaves, he brings up Friday night. He invited us to spend the night at his house. Working out. Bonding. Watching wrestling movies. I been looking forward to it.

"Ya still invited. A part of the team."

Coach is gone before third period bell rings. When the fifth period bell goes off, I take another spot on another mat, leaving a big, wet stain where I was.

Two thirty. Four periods later, I'm opening the door. The team gonna come soon. Don't wanna see 'em. Or nobody.

Leaving the building, my coat in my locker — my purse and books there, too.

"Autumn!" Roberto's wheelchair hops the curb. He moving in between kids and buses, trying to get to me. He don't listen to teachers trying to stop him. His long, stringy black hair blowing into his eyes. "Autumn. Do you want this?"

He holding up another present. A long box wrapped in pretty, hot-pink paper.

I'm close enough to pick it out his hand like it's a leaf. Backing up, shaking my head, I don't say one word. I run.

Cutting through trees, up the hill, I pick up speed.

Snow gets inside my sneakers. Falling off branches, it drops onto my back. Cold, wet air cuts my arms and cheeks after I been at it a while. Everything is burning. My fingers. Cheeks. My frozen toes. Can't hardly feel my arms.

I don't stop, though. I keep at it. Running and wrestling make me feel strong, perfect, powerful. Can't nobody understand. As ain't everything.

CHAPTER 30

ADONIS

Her black shorts would show everything, but her purple tights are good at keeping secrets. "You ever been bad at anything?" Autumn asks me.

It's a ridiculous question. If you prepare, practice, you can absolutely avoid screwing up. "No." I sit a book on the table. It was shelved incorrectly.

"Nothing?" She looks up at me, almost smiling. She does not do that much anymore.

"Autumn." I've been trying to be patient with her. Ma helped me understand. It's difficult losing something of importance to you, even if you were responsible. "I try to prepare, to make sure that I do everything the right way the first time. So I . . ." I want to say that goof ups happen when you are immature and running around thinking that life is all fun and games. Ma says

I sound like an old man when I speak this way. I think I sound wise. Wisdom keeps you from making errors and mistakes.

Moving to the next bookshelf, I keep my thoughts to myself. Autumn does not really care to hear them anyway.

Walking beside me, she picks at her hair. No feathers. I thought feathers were a silly look for a girl her age. She has not worn one lately, not since leaving the team three weeks ago. I am not sure I like this new look.

She always seems to be thinking now. Introspective and quiet. That's disconcerting. I never thought I would say that I'd rather hear her talking foolishness, saying nonsensical things. Laughing for no reason. At least I'd know what she was thinking.

"Adonis." She pulls a book from the shelf, not for any reason, though. "How many years it take to get from here to Jupiter?" She looks at the ceiling, like she can see the constellations. "See . . . that's how long it seem like it's gonna take me . . . to learn to . . . read on grade level."

Tears come. Plenty. Almost every day now.

I look away. I do not know what to do when it happens.

"I been reading like this for so long. . . ." She sniffs, wiping her nose on the back of her hand, like the guys at practice. "Messing up in school since second grade . . ."

Pushing past her, I feel my eyes water. Stopping, I realize that I cannot be around her anymore. I love libraries. Books are sacred to me, fun. I escape in them. Lately, before I come to volunteer, I worry: Will she cry today? Should I avoid pressing her to do her work? What if she crawls onto my lap? What should I do?

I think I may switch my volunteer days. Or work at the public library instead. It all makes me furious. The world does not revolve around Autumn.

". . . Stuck."

I look over my shoulder, trying to understand what she means.

"I'm stuck." Pointing to a plastic palm tree in a pot, she says, "Like that . . . there." Her parents thought they could afford to pay to get her extra reading help at night. It's so expensive, they cannot afford it.

She walks over to the tree, sticking her arms out like branches. She sits on the floor, knocking on the hard plastic pot. "Stuck." She hasn't been attending class, I know. Miss Baker came in one day to speak with her. Mr. Epperson, as well. It's hilarious, I think, that a girl who hates books and libraries makes sure to volunteer twice a week. Even when she does not go to class.

"Autumn . . ."

"You ever feel stuck?"

Swallowing, I sit up tall.

"Adonis." She walks over, kneeling at my wheels. "People be so fake." Her head lowers, so I cannot see she's crying. "Maybe I'm not smart. But I'm truthful." Her mother says she tells people too much about herself. "I can't read. . . . I say it. What's wrong with that?" She keeps talking. "I been thinking . . . sometimes . . . in this chair . . ."

"Autumn . . ."

"Roberto say sometimes he feel like me . . . stuck . . ."

I ask her why she is talking to a seventh grader about things that are personal to her. "It's his business," I say, "how he feels about being disabled, sitting in a chair. Quit asking people things like that." She is holding on to my chair handles, crying again. How can I move? I'm stuck, too. "Autumn —"

She thinks it's a good question to ask and she apologizes if I think that it's not. She has never apologized for anything she has done to me. And she has done a lot. "Why you don't like to talk, Adonis?"

Mrs. Carolyn calls us both.

"You are talking about me." I back up. "I am an excellent student with outstanding grades. You should be thinking about yourself, Autumn Knight."

Standing up, walking beside me, she informs me that she has been thinking of herself. "That's why I ain't been to class so much. To see what the right thing to do is, I gotta think."

I think all the time — at home in the den, at night in my bed, in the van on the way to school. Even on the toilet. My mind is constantly examining and studying the world and people around me. "Autumn, you are making your situation worse. Getting further behind in class will not help you to read better."

"I know."

We take the elevator to the second floor of the library. "Then why . . . oh, forget it," I say.

She is not a girl who thinks logically. She has me wasting my voice, my time.

"If we got stuck in this elevator —"

"Quit talking about being stuck!" I point to her. "Do what you are supposed to do!" She has me yelling. "And you will have everything you want in life!"

I point at her again and again. "It's your fault. Start

there. Quit complaining. If you need to read better, get better. Get help. Ask someone. People want people to succeed. No one wants to see you fail."

When the door opens, with her rushing out, I think I will never see Autumn Knight again. Good.

Leaving the library, she is so close that her jacket button taps my chair. Classes are changing. It's very crowded in the hall. She sprays on perfume, the same scent she wore the day she sat in my lap.

"Adonis Einstein Anderson Miller."

Only Ma uses my full name. "Yes, Autumn."

Taking a deep breath, she says, "Will you help me learn to read better?"

I know the people around us must have heard her question, especially my honors English teacher, who is walking just ahead of us. She looks over her shoulder at Autumn and me, and smiles. Of course Autumn doesn't care. She believes that everyone is exactly like her, waving their lives in front of the whole world like dirty laundry.

How can I say no, without my honors English teacher thinking less of me?

CHAPTER 31

Autumn

$\mathcal{M}$e and Peaches cooking. Arguing over math, too, and the cheat sheet she tried to give me recently. "But I ain't ask you for it."

"Well —" She puts sticks of butter in the pot, stirring. "I was helping you out anyhow."

I stop rolling out dough. "You thinking I'm stupid, too? Everybody thinking that, huh?" I rush across the kitchen, pulling open the drawer. POOR GRADES TAKE DOWN STAR WRESTLER, the newspaper article say. "It's not right. Schools should keep a kid's private stuff private."

Peaches look at me for a long time. Before she say anything, I'm telling her, "I fail on my own. Pass that way, too." I open the window. Tear up the article, let the wind have it.

We both go back to work. Sweating like we in the

oven baking with those apple pies. We cooking for the lady up the block. She got book club today. Twenty chicken potpies. Six apple pies. Plus lemon berry ice cream. Everything from scratch, even the ice cream.

Pressing out the dough, I think about Adonis. He shoulda said yes, I'll help you read better. Two days passed already. Why ain't he say nothing?

Peaches walking over, blowing a spoon filled with veggies and chicken. I open my mouth, wide. "A little more pepper, this much salt." I show her with my fingers. I take the top off the pot. Watch the chicken pushing past the peas, the carrots sitting on top the string beans while I think about that article. They used to write good things about me.

Getting back to the table, Peaches start up with school again.

She and me never talked about her cheating. Not the first time. Not the second time after she tried to pass me that paper. Then she did it again yesterday. Like I didn't already show her that's not something I do. "Do you want to pass ninth grade?" She rolling a piece of dough in her hand, eating it. "You getting further and further behind." If I just catch up on a few tests, she saying, I'll feel better about myself.

I yank open the cabinet. "So cheat. That's what you want me to do?"

I got some nerve acting high and mighty, she saying, when I'm practically flunking school. I wanna know how she can cheat and talk about wanting to be the twelfth-grade valedictorian when the time come. Three times don't make her a cheat. She telling me that without laughing at herself.

I'm at the cabinet, pushing boxes and cans around, looking for vanilla and lemon extract for these pies. That's when I see it written on a can. Big and red. All the letters capitalized. EVAPORATED. It's how I feel. Invisible, almost gone.

Running upstairs, holding on to the can, I open my jar. Spelling the word out in pearl-gray crayon. I stuff the paper in the jar and put the lid back on.

Peaches calling me. I'm Google searching, looking for a definition for evaporate. *Vanish. Fade*, one site says. I like those. "No, this the one I like." I mix my definition with theirs, like grits and butter. *Evaporate* is . . . when all the moisture in you or something else is dried out and nothing's left behind but the solid stuff. Everything else done vanished.

"Autumn! I can't make pies!"

My mother calling me now, right along with Peaches, like I been up here forever.

Walking downstairs, I'm thinking. This how I been feeling — like my body is here but the inside of me is fading. Evaporated. Sucked away. Gone, like wrestling.

"Dad!" My father's got a spoon dipping in the pot, sampling our food.

"You gonna get that restaurant, I do believe." Kissing my cheek, he reminds me I gotta save some of the money I make for the books I threw away. They wasn't free to the libraries that bought 'em. So I have to pay 'em back.

Mom's behind him, mentioning Miss Baker. She called late last night. I skipped her class all week and would be on punishment, but the book club asked us to cook three months ago. We can't let 'em down. And what else my parents gonna take away from me? Cooking?

Miss Pattie walking into the kitchen, dressed in all red, talking about school. She got this idea. She will work with me on my reading. "Four hours every Saturday. That'll do it."

We arguing, 'cause my parents like what she saying. Peaches and me yelling 'cause that's our cooking day. Plus I'm thinking Miss Pattie gonna give me eczema like she gave Peaches, bugging me about school all the time.

When Peaches's father walks in using a cane, everybody gets quiet. If wrinkles was wings, he could fly to Paris, I think. "Peaches." He walks over to her. "Studying time." Looking at his watch, he say they need to leave.

Miss Pattie got to remind him that we cooking. "Running a business." Then she whispers, "He getting old."

She take him back to the living room and then comes in reminding the two of us. "Study. Do well in school. A girl needs that."

I wonder sometimes, with all her talk, if Miss Pattie don't feel like she evaporating, too.

CHAPTER 32

ADONIS

Ma knows my secrets. For instance, I sleep in the nude. I like the food in our refrigerator to be in nice, neat rows: pickles, mayonnaise, apple juice. They must be lined up one behind the other. Not alphabetically — mentally ill people do that. There is one more thing about me. I do not like to fail at anything.

I could never teach Autumn to read. Not that I'd want to. If I did, it wouldn't work out. Autumn is . . . Ma says I might want to quit calling her lazy. The other day I also used the *D* word. That disappointed Ma. I hate to disappoint her.

I think Autumn knows that I will not — cannot help her. She came into the media center today, and barely spoke to me. Mrs. Carolyn is meeting with her now. You cannot volunteer at the library and skip classes. Or come to class late and neglect to hand in your homework. I know what she's been up to. Miss Baker is in here a lot, discussing Autumn's behavior. Mrs. Carolyn defends Autumn. "A library is a sanctuary," she told Miss Baker the other day. "The students who come here . . . don't need to be perfect."

Autumn is enjoying herself a little too much, Miss Baker said. That is funny to hear. Autumn is sad a lot. But she comes, even when she isn't volunteering.

The two of them are in the back room. I am watching the front desk, eavesdropping, which is something I don't normally do.

"People have been extremely patient with you. . . ." Mrs. Carolyn wants Autumn to keep volunteering. But that's impossible, she says, if she refuses to participate in her own education. "It's not like you. . . ." She's asking her over and over again, what she or Miss Baker or anyone here can do to get her back on track. "We're afraid, sweetie . . . your grades next semester will be even worse."

If Autumn is talking, I cannot hear her. But it's unfair. A girl with her grades and habits has everyone chasing after her, begging her to be better and to do better.

Ralph walks over, carrying books. "I can check you out," I say. He hands me books to return as well. A biography of George Washington and *Manchild in the Promised Land*. I rush him off. "Return them in three weeks."

Mrs. Carolyn asks her again, what is going on? "Do you think this behavior will get you back on the team? Are you striking?"

Autumn laughs. "I think, Mrs. Carolyn . . . I ain't volunteering here no more."

Mrs. Carolyn is not expecting that. She follows Autumn into the main area. "I hate to see you go . . . but . . ." She hugs Autumn and lets her know that she may use the media center whenever she likes. Autumn asks if she may stay the period. "It's your lunch period. Come every day during this time and read or —"

Autumn walks away. Taking a seat beside me, she explains everything I've heard.

"You gonna miss me?"

Is she asking or telling me?

Leaning on one elbow, she stares into my eyes. It's been a long time since she has done that. *"Firstly,"* she says. "I still remember what that means."

I'm surprised.

"Firstly . . ." She reaches past me, picking up the book *The Autobiography of Malcolm X,* and sits it back down. "That's a movie, ain't it?"

"Yes."

Shaking her head up and down, she asks how many hours I study a day. "As many as I need to." Swallowing, I think about her question. I hope she does not ask me again to help her read.

Taking paper from her pocket and unfolding it, she shows it to me. "*Stuck*." It's her new word. If she tells me something, can I keep it to myself, she'd like to know.

"Yes."

She has a jar — at her age — with words in it. Only a few. She whispers words into my ear. *Quandary. Quibble. Quaint.* Who doesn't know what those mean? I ask, feeling uncomfortable.

Walking over to the dictionary, turning pages slowly, she says, "Come here, Adonis."

I am working. She calls me three more times.

"I like this meaning . . . it fits me."

"*Definition*. You mean you like the *definition*."

Sitting beside her, I read in my head while she reads aloud. "Stuck. Jammed. Im . . . mov . . . able." She runs her finger under each word. "This problem's got me completely stuck."

She's brought this word up before. *Stuck*. It's not as if I'd want it to happen, but other words pop into my mind as well. *Trapped. Wedged. Pinned.* In the pond, I couldn't escape. Not on my own. Later they found my chair, wedged between an abandoned car and vacant house. Smashed with hammers.

She folds and slides the paper into her pocket, walking to a table to sit down. Then jumping up, riffling through magazines, she carries a handful over to her seat, humming. Then I get a text.

U gonna teach me 2 read better?

It takes me a minute to decide to delete the message. Afterward, I go back to work.

Teachers here depend on me. I cannot be distracted by every single little thing. Autumn Knight should know that.

CHAPTER 33

Autumn

I quit the library 'cause. I just quit, that's all.
Loving him is in me forever and always, like
the blood in my veins. It's just that I'm all mixed up.
Baffled. Stuck in places nobody can see. It ain't just
wrestling that got me this way. I'm stuck in love with
Adonis, who don't care 'bout me not one bit — even me
reading better.

I'm stuck back on a sixth-grade reading level, while
everybody else is moving ahead fast as Harry Potter on
that train.

"Keep this up," Mom said this morning, playing
back messages from my teachers, "and you won't never
graduate."

Six weeks done passed. How many times I been to
vice principal's office?

People see me at school laughing on the phone. Inside I am on the mat. Squashed. Not able to get up. Teachers, what do they know? Opponents ain't all in the circle or sitting next to you in class. They inside you, slowing you down. Some days I think — I should drop out.

Looking over my shoulder. Staring at Adonis. I put my head down so he don't see me spying.

Seeing Peaches's father again the other day, finalized my mind. Married when you don't want to be. Forced to stay when you wanna go. Stuck. Me making Adonis stick to me when he don't want to. Fourteen years old used to be easy, I bet.

"Zup, Autumn."

I make room for Jaxxon. "Hey."

"You not working?" He plucks my magazine, leaning over, laying his head on the table. He staring up, smiling. "Oh, I forgot. You got fired."

He works, he says. Doing a little something something for a teacher after school. But I shouldn't ask, Jaxxon say, 'cause he not gonna tell who he is. He so stupid, I gotta laugh.

"You dropped out?" he asking, like I'm not in school right here, pushing his arm off my shoulder. "Mr. E. got people looking for you, Autumn."

"What?" I was in his class yesterday. This morning . . . I had a headache.

Jaxxon got his hands on my wrist. "He told us . . . bring her in . . . anyway . . . anyhow."

Laughing, pulling my hand loose from his, I ask if he crazy.

Adonis pass by. Jaxxon following him with his eyes. "That dude don't never have any fun." He bending back the ends of my magazine. Sitting quiet, sitting close, he asking me to the movies.

I'm laughing, 'cause I don't like him like that. Me and him too much alike. He say, "Peaches and you. Y'all both cute. Let me see your cell phone."

He not calling her from my phone, I say. Then right before I leave, I remember the B he got in math the other day. "How you do it? Cheat? I won't tell. . . . Sometimes you just gotta do that, I guess." I think about Peaches. We got our third-quarter midterm grades. She got a A in math so far this quarter. Maybe I really am stupid. Everybody else in that class cheating. Honest Autumn, failing every test.

Raven walking by, waving. Jaxxon leave for a little while. Coming back, he can't stop smiling. "Got her number." He holding it up, waving. "Cute girl like her" — he kisses air — "need somebody."

Shoving him, I ask why he always putting on, chasing girls who could care less about him. He give it back to me, pointing at Adonis. "And he want you?"

Both of us sitting with our arms on our legs, looking across the room at him. "No." I say it out loud. So I'll believe it, too.

Changing the subject, I ask about Mr. E. "He still getting that operation? Don't need it. He a little too skinny now."

Jaxxon shaking his head, asking why a girl who can beat boys wrestling can't see when a teacher lying to her.

CHAPTER 34

ADONIS

Mr. Epperson asked if I would help a struggling student. Someone with potential, who cannot seem to grasp the fundamentals of algebra. I said I would see if I could help. Mr. Epperson has been a little under the weather.

"Good morning, Mr. Epperson." I move at his pace, following him into the library. Six of his students are sitting at a table. Raven and two guys from my AP statistics class are here to tutor as well. State tests are coming up. Mr. Epperson swears that with all the brainpower in our honors and AP programs, we can help improve the scores of struggling students at our school as quickly as any teacher.

He gives each student their marching orders. They disperse throughout the library along with their tutees.

I am all set to ask which student he wants me to work with, when he points toward her. She is slouched in a black beanbag over by the wall, her back facing us.

I freeze.

Autumn has not spoken much to me lately. At the library, she talks to her new friends. They've taken to really liking it here: eating their lunches in the caf, and then loafing in the library three or four days a week. Laughing. They do a lot of that.

She wasn't expecting me. When I say hello, she practically jumps out of her skin. Tiny papers in her lap fall to the floor like confetti. "Adonis." Looking over at Mr. Epperson, she reaches down. "You don't have to help me." She picks up her red jacket, folding it in two. "I know you don't want to." Standing up again, she looks around, for another place to sit, I think.

She has a notebook and a ruddy pencil. Most students have their math books here as well. When she sees my eyes on the things in her hands, she squeezes them to her chest. "I ain't want to come anyway. . . ."

I'm thinking about what she told me once. *Ain't* is her favorite word.

She picks at the feather in her hair. She's back to wearing feathers. "Mr. E. promised me" — she turns around, with her head high — "extra-credit points."

Moving quickly, I try to keep up with her. My eyes stay glued to her legs. Her purple tights disappear under her short gray skirt like smoke in the sky. Her curls dangle from her head like black, shiny ribbons. Stopping, sitting in my chair in the middle of the media center, I ask myself, *Why would I ever chase after Autumn Knight?*

There is a dictionary to my right. I'm pretending to riffle through it when I notice her name carved on the wooden stand. I look at Mrs. Carolyn and then Autumn, who is almost at the door. *Undisciplined.* She ought to look that up. *Careless. Irresponsible.* Those are good words for her to learn. When I see my full name written underneath hers in calligraphy, with a plus sign in between, my head practically explodes.

I am a private person. Something like this — written for everyone to see — is not me. A girl like her . . . is not me. For me. If she knew me, she would know this.

I hear her black heels on the linoleum by the front door. Tapping like hammers on nails, they walk her out into the hall. I am wondering what to do about my name, when I hear tapping again. Her shoes. Her voice — saying hello to Raven, cheery and high. From the moment she returns, her eyes are on mine. She looks upset. What nerve.

"Adonis." Her hands go to her hips.

Raven passes by, staring.

"Autumn, why did you — ?"

We are both talking at once. Turning pages in the dictionary, I ignore her. I stop at the *P*s, my finger jabbing the page. I ask if she can read that word. *"Privacy."* As clearly as I am able, I explain how she has violated my right to privacy by writing my full name on this desk. I do not expect her to apologize.

Practically falling into my lap, she turns more pages. She finds her own word. *Apologize*. She writes the word down. I watch her put the letter *I* in front of it. Not saying a word, as if she left her voice in the hallway along with her notebook and jacket, she finds other words: *Disappointed. Mad. Sad.*

She closes the dictionary carefully, rubbing it as if it were a magic stone. "You don't like me, Adonis. I know that now." She breathes in deep. "And not 'cause you treated me mean . . . or ran from me all those times." She steps out of her heels, holding them in her hands. "I know 'cause when I asked you to help me with my reading, you ain't say yes. You ain't say no."

If I had said yes, it would have meant I wanted her to do better, she says. Had I said no, it would mean to forget it, "Get somebody else to help you." Not to acknowledge her request meant "You don't care if I sink or swim."

Her shoes move from hand to hand. Her feet stay put. Her orange toenails, painted with white dots, look like springtime, not winter outside, freezing everything.

"If I saw you at that pond, Adonis . . . I woulda jumped in and saved you. Even if I ain't know how to swim."

Stepping closer to me, her knees touch the edge of my chair, like they did in my dream. She stoops. "But I been thinking lately. . . ."

I smell baby powder when she sits her shoes on the floor.

"I'm good at swimming. I ever told you that?"

She leans forward, taking a deep breath — kissing me.

My back stiffens.

Her mouth opens.

My hands, limp in my lap, are as cold as the metal they made my chair with.

Tasting peppermint.

Feeling her fingers, smooth and soft on my cheeks.

I kiss her.

And let her sweetness in.

Pulling away, Autumn takes my first ever kiss with her.

"Good-bye, Adonis."

I swallow. The students around us shout and cheer.

Autumn and those shoes walk out of the library. This time, she does not come back.

ESCAPE

Sometime at school I escape by looking out the window at clouds. Or watching Peaches do calligraphy or cooking — things like that.

Wrestlers escape too — all the time. But on the mat, we can't have our minds all up in the clouds.

Let me paint a picture for you. Pretend I'm on my hands and knees on the mat. Can you see my opponent, kneeling on one knee close beside me; arms in position? Good. I'm in what's called the bottom position. My opponent in the top position.

Escaping means I break physical contact and arm control with my opponent. Then I stand face-to-face with 'em, in the neutral position. It ain't easy. He want to score and win, too. So my opponent will do what he or she got to do, within bounds to stop me. But I'm a tough competitor. I don't give up easy.

CHAPTER 35

Autumn

*Y*ou can be thinking a boy is your everything. Till he let you down. Then you be wondering how you ever liked him in the first place.

I try to forget that boy. His lips. How when he kissed me back, my insides warmed up like a restaurant full of candles. It's hard. I love him.

I'm at the library, near my house. Texted Peaches, asked if she wanted to go to the mall. Her dad went to the hospital last night. Congestive heart failure. She home watching him. I'm here 'cause it's not far from my house. And Mom wouldn't drive me nowhere else.

The public library round our way ain't big. The statue of Frederick Douglass standing out front is. Holding a book, he stares down at you, with hair long as a woman's, wild as a lion's.

Never did I like that big, gray metal statue. Those eyes. They look at you accusingly-like. In seventh grade during a field trip, the librarian told us Mr. Douglass's eyes be asking people questions: "Can you do what I've done? Travel the road I walked?"

Maybe those ain't her exact same words. But they close.

A woman, walking by me, looking up at him, too. "Love his book."

I keep walking.

"Narrative of the Life of Frederick Douglass. Ever read it?"

I'm shaking my head no, wondering why I'm here at the library, when school is out and I don't wanna read or do homework or nothing.

"It would be a pleasure to show you where to find it."

She's got me by the arm, like she know me. Pushing open the door, telling me stuff about herself. She just got out of library school. She went to Spelman College, she says. Mrs. Carolyn graduated from there. She the new librarian. Her first day was last Thursday. They wanna start a teen group soon. Maybe I wanna join it, she say. "Or help me form it. Whatdaya say?"

She talking a lot, moving fast. Her clothes look African. But she look like my cousin: cool sunglasses, fake nails, and a eyebrow pierced. She wanna know my name.

"Autumn Knight."

Her hoop earrings patting the sides of her face while she bending down near her desk. Saying my name sound familiar. "Oh." Shaking my hand, she winks. "The wrestler."

"How you know me?"

Smiling, she say she reads everything. "Hold a sec." After she helps a few people, she pulls out a file on me — not just the articles they wrote on me this year. She got other ones. Even from when I first started. "Research," she saying, "my favorite part of the job."

I wonder if she kept those bad articles they wrote about me. She moving every second, it seem. Helping this person. On the computer hunting for books or articles for somebody else. Still talking to me.

When a lady and her kids come looking for Keena Ford books, she walks 'em over to the kiddie section.

I sneak upstairs, turn on the computer, and watch videos. Something is different up here now. Can't tell what. I don't itch. Maybe that's it. Last time my teacher had to call home because my skin was on fire, my nose dripping. I got to leave early that day and not read out loud like the other kids.

Bored, I'm walking downstairs, looking for the magazine section. I thumb through a copy of *Wrestling USA*. Looking at pictures, I think of me on the mat. It make me sad. Thinking about that kiss. Adonis kissing me back. Makes me sadder.

I'm shaking my head to get him outta my mind. But my heart, he always gonna be there. Like that extra beat the doctors say my grandmother got. I'm turning pages, reading with my fingers, underlining words that way. I stop. Borrowing a pen, I write down two words for my jar. *Discipline. Self-confidence.* Wrestling give you that. It says it right here. Coach always told us wrestling will strengthen you inside and out, "on the mat and in the world."

Did it help me . . . outside the gym? Maybe . . . when it came to chasing Adonis. I was disciplined 'bout that. *What about cooking?* I always did that. When I was eight, even.

School . . . discipline . . . me . . . ? No. Reading. Forget it. Since I saw him on Tuesday, I been thinking and thinking, *How do smart kids get all those As? Is Peaches smarter than me? Miss Pattie be pushing her. If she didn't . . . would she still do better in school?*

Competition. Mr. E. was talking 'bout that again yesterday. I think some kids compete against everybody in class. They never gonna be outdone. It's the mat and the frying pan that bring out the beast in me.

I text Peaches, asking about Mr. E.

I couldn't sleep the night I gave Adonis that kiss. Stayed up half the night making macaroons. Gave them to Mr. E. yesterday. I don't think he'll eat them. No appetite lately, that's what he said.

Looking out the window, watching pigeons sitting on Mr. Douglass's head, I try my best to push Adonis out my mind. A boy with no legs. *Why you want him?* Peaches be saying. Why not?

I gotta do better. Come up with a plan like I do during wrestling season. Run every day. Lift weights. Eat small portions. No snacks. Be ready to win. That's why it's hard to beat me on the mat. *Was* hard. Folding my words, putting 'em in my wallet, I think about my jar filling up. I put my first *W* word in it. *Wallaby*. Seen a show on television about them.

Laying my head down, shutting my eyes, I feel his lips on mine again. Did he kiss another girl before? Raven? Do he like my lips on his? I don't want to think them things or think about him. I'm working hard not to. *Wallaby, wallaby, wallaby.*

"Uh. Excuse me. Are you that girl?"

I sit up. "What girl?"

"The wrestler. Yeah. I see your muscles."

He pull up a chair, talking a mile a minute. He's in high school. His sister wants to wrestle. She read about me in the paper. Only she eleven and her school don't have a team. He been teaching her. He hold up two wrestling books. "We need some pointers. Things she can do every day."

"Jump rope. It's good for you, and little girls like to do it anyhow." I tell him that running gives wrestlers stamina. Once a month on Saturdays, he come here looking over the new magazines, or checking out a new book, he say. "She's going to the Olympics." He ask if I'm going. "You should."

His name is Michael. He walks here, lives only four blocks away. "You studying?" He talk a lot. "Bet you a good student, huh?" He leaning back in his seat, profiling. "Girls be like that, rocking those As. Making us look bad."

Wishing he would go away.

His sister would love to talk to me, he saying, pulling out his cell and dialing her. He give me the phone after she gets on. She screaming. "You a superstar to her," he say, leaving.

I go a little while later myself. Making it past the librarian is easy. She in the stacks, picking books off the shelf, excited 'bout helping somebody with a book report, a kid my age. I hear her say *The Color Purple*'s a good book. Then she mention some book about skin.

Jogging by the statue, looking up again, I ask Mr. Douglass a question. "How you read so good? Way back then, when I can't do it now?"

CHAPTER 36

ADONIS

"A donis Miller. Clean that up, please."

It's the second beaker I've broken this week. Sweeping broken glass into a dustpan, I try not to listen to the students sitting around me. Raven, however, is loud and clear, when she says, "I'm so glad he isn't my partner."

I am disciplined. Focused. I always think before I act. Lately, I don't know. I am not very careful.

Mr. Epperson has invited me to work with his class again. So following honors biology, I head into his room. I am looking forward to it. The principal knows that I've taught in there a few times. He chastised Mr. Epperson, even though he's sick.

"A teacher who never breaks the rules," Mr. Epperson

says, "might need to wonder if they're supposed to be teaching in the first place."

Having a good relationship with the principal is essential. I need him to write college recommendations, refer me for summer jobs with state officials so people there know the kind of student I am.

But Mr. Epperson. When I get in front of his class, I know I was born to teach.

When I get to Mr. Epperson's class, I sit my hall pass on his desk and get to work immediately, explaining things. This period I have art class. Since I'm ahead of everyone else, my teacher allows me to come here. She and Mr. Epperson made a pact: For some very expensive South American coffee, she will allow me to come here every now and then. I think he owes her a few bags.

From the front of the class, I can see everything. Nose pickers. Sleepyheads. Whisperers.

I see Patricia jabbing Autumn in the side while I teach. Whispering. Most likely she is discussing me. One concern I have is that Autumn will tell someone that I've kissed her. What would be worse than people believing that she is my girlfriend?

I work with the class for twenty minutes. Afterward

I take a few questions. Surprisingly, Jaxxon is sitting up, hatless.

"Papers out, folks. Pencils, too." On my way out, Mr. Epperson asks me to wait in the hall. He'd like to speak with me.

Everyone is starting to notice how thin he's getting. A little tired, too. Usually he stands while I talk. This time he stayed seated. He hasn't said anything to anyone, Mrs. Carolyn says. But people are wondering.

While Autumn's class takes their quiz, he and I talk about a summer research project. He knows this college professor. "It will be challenging, but — you're smart enough to help him out."

Standing next to me, he puts his hand on my shoulder. "Of course I'll do it." Swallowing, I ask if he needs me to do anything for him. "Grade homework. Anything. You name it, Mr. Epperson."

He heads back inside, coughing.

I am at the elevator when I get asked for my hall pass. I left it on Mr. Epperson's desk. The substitute teacher suggests that I go back to get it.

From outside of his class, I can see Autumn scratching her head. Patricia, cheating. I am not surprised. There's a cheat sheet on her thigh. She's scribbling, looking down, and then up, checking to see if Mr. Epperson is watching. It's too much. I'm sure that's why she doesn't notice me.

Autumn is being Autumn, writing and erasing. *An honest failure beats a lying win,* I think.

"Mr. Epperson."

Patricia's thighs close as fast and tight as a dungeon door. She looks at me. She knows.

Cheaters ruin it for everyone. They mess up the curve. Plus, it's dishonest. "May I speak to you outside, sir?"

You cannot let things like this pass. It even hurts the cheater if you don't speak up.

"Yeah, Adonis."

"I came back for my pass."

Both her hands are on her desk. Her legs are crossed, and shaking.

He brings it to me. I feel bad, since he seems out of breath.

"Something else, sir . . . I came back to say . . . to speak to you about . . ."

"I'm administering a test, Adonis."

"Mr. Epperson . . ." It's unlike me to run out of words. "I need to speak to you about . . . about . . ."

He looks at his watch. "Can this wait?"

I leave the room. Thinking about Patricia, I stop. *I have the evidence,* I think to myself. Last year, she did get that test from them. She was going to cheat.

My watch, I unbuckle it and touch the impression on my skin. *My own cousin would let me drown,* I think.

CHAPTER 37

Autumn

*O*kay, Peaches!"

"Let me explain it to you again, Autumn."

"No. I got a headache." Closing my books, I walk away from the table, ignoring her when she say I better get my butt back over there.

Why did I ask her for help? She made the answer too complicated. Now I'm confused all over again.

Picking up a bowl of pickles, I cross the cafeteria, eating 'em one by one. I'll shape our pickles like flowers when we own a restaurant.

"Hey." Jaxxon stands beside me. "Smile."

I give him a fake one.

"What's wrong with you?"

"Nothing." Looking around, I see Roberto and wave.

I'm finally keeping my promise to him, letting him teach me to play chess in the library today after school.

"Don't wave." Jaxxon looks at Adonis. He telling me about the time he asked him for help studying for a algebra test.

"Did you pass it?"

"Did awright," he says, watching girls walk by. " 'Cause of Mr. Epperson working with me, not him."

I am not going to wave at Adonis. But I'm staring. "How come you don't wear suits?"

He stares down at his jeans. "I don't wanna look like him."

I'm sorta dressed up myself today. A skirt and top — plus my feather. Peaches yells for me. Jaxxon tells me to go to my mother. Walking over to our table, I pick up my books. "I'm not mad," I say to her. "Just leaving."

In the library, upstairs, way in the back, I sit by myself. Doing nothing for a long time. Bored with math, with reading. I turn on my phone and watch some matches. We made it to states. I woulda, too. Going over the moves in my head while they making 'em on the mat, I get sad. Then I take myself over to the stacks and sit down.

Pulling out a book. Any book. Looking at the pictures. Laughing at one that got ladies wearing corsets and men with long, scraggily beards, I take a picture and text it to Peaches. This yr husband, I write.

"Sorry," she say, "for being Pattie today."

The bell rings. I slide between the stacks, evaporating into the books, looking over the thin ones. Something about the old ones I like sometimes, not the smell or the faded pages but the type and all those big words, not that I understand 'em. Lying on the floor, under the sun, eyes closed. I wake up and he's staring down at me.

"Do you have class, Autumn?"

I flatten my skirt. "I was thinking . . . they won't miss me."

Usually Adonis be trying to escape, running as fast as he can. Staying put, he keeps looking at me. I'm wondering what he thinks, what he sees. But I stand up anyhow. "See you."

It's not till I'm on the first floor that I start breathing again. Green is for sure his color. It make his eyes pop.

Finding another corner, in the back, on the first floor. In the empty library computer room, I open my reading book. Biting my thumbnail, I read in my head, telling myself over and over again, "You can do it. Keep trying. Don't quit."

CHAPTER 38

ADONIS

Roberto! Nate! Stop it!"

Their wheelchairs crash into each other. Like gladiators riding chariots into battle, they swing rulers and sticks, striking each other on the heads, poking shoulder blades and elbows. "Cut it out!" I rush into the hall, wedging my wheel in the door, practically falling out of the chair.

More seventh graders show up, steering their wheels toward the fight. They push and roll as fast as they are able. Spinning and bumping, yelling and hitting, the five of them ignore my pleas. "Marvin, didn't I —"

It's springtime. Everyone, even a few of the teachers, are acting out of sorts. Marvin's hands are on his wheels, moving them back and forth. Like a race-car driver revving up his engine, he finally takes off. A boy a few feet from him does the same, pushing, rolling as fast as they can, while the other boys cheer. Turning their wheels just before impact, they crash wheels. Marvin flies out of his seat, and onto the floor — landing by a classroom door, he laughs. Roberto has to help him up. Since he has fallen out his chair, he will lose points, Roberto reminds him.

The other boys begin to finger their wheels. I take things into my own hands. Backing up, bracing myself, I ram my chair into the thick of them. Pulling Roberto by the collar, I issue a stern warning. "This is a school. Behave yourselves. Or else."

Apparently they were playing a game, and not fighting. But they are here for chess club. "Not to dillydally around," I say, ushering them into the room.

"Did you ever play that game?" Roberto asks me.

Of course I haven't. Someone could get hurt.

Marvin looks at the board, contemplating his next move. "My cousin's electric chair moves fast. Zoom," he says, slapping his hands together. "I could win against everyone in that."

The chatter starts up again. Chess pieces become airplanes, wheelchairs, and cars. Holding them up in the air, they ask if I think about driving, sometimes. Or getting legs. "I want a pair," CK says, and adds he doesn't know why, but playing chess isn't something he wants to do today. "When I get 'em, I'm racing in the Olympics." He bumps fists with Roberto.

Two of the other young men have legs. A bullet paralyzed one boy. The other was in a car crash. They look at me, asking again about legs. "If you would like to have them, and can afford to get them," I say, "then you should. I — like myself this way." I stop and remember that it's true. I love my body. I love being me. When I dream, I forget.

Before I realize it, two hours have passed. Hardly any chess has been played. The entire time the boys tell me about their game. Sometimes a wheelchair falls over; a student ends up on the ground. It has gotten them nearly suspended twice. I've never heard of the game. They made it up. It's called Wheel Crash.

When chess club ends, I hand Roberto a laptop. I've been tutoring him regularly for months now. I almost gave it to him earlier. But I wanted him to appreciate learning for its own sake, not for the price at the end.

He's a quick study. His grades are rising fast. "This is for you." I've used my own money to have it restored and cleaned. His name is engraved across the top in silver.

Running his fingers over the letters, Roberto smiles at me. "Wow." His friends, gathering around like baby ducks, ask if I could tutor them as well. When they leave, they bring up their game again. It's fun. I should learn to play, they say, on their way out.

Waiting outside the school for Ma, I watch Roberto and his friends still horsing around. They toss book bags and punches. They text girls in their classes, while they wait on the van, which is late. Roberto pushes his way over to me. "Adonis." He giggles into his hand. "If . . . we start a secret club, will you be the president?"

Before I can answer, he says they will call it the Wheel Crashers Club Number One.

I've always played by the rules. I could never for one moment be in charge of something the school is against. Roberto will understand when he is older. Autumn never would. At weigh-ins one day, leaning into me, quietly she asked if I ever do anything wrong.

I was too exhausted to be upset with her. I'd woken up at four to finish a project, tutored some students at school at seven thirty before going to class, and worked with the wrestling team later.

As soon as the boys are picked up, I get a text from Ma. She's running late. I head for the library until it closes, wondering why Autumn is in here.

Autumn sits at a desk, with her shoes off. Her toes grip the side of the desk, while her teeth chew on a pencil. Books would be piled up around me if I were here late. She has a notebook in front of her, and a text-book — which is closed.

Opening the book, she makes a face. A few seconds later, she's scratching, tapping her pencil on the table. It's math. I just bet that's what she's working on.

"Hi, Mrs. —"

"Shhh," Mrs. Carolyn says, pointing toward Autumn. "This is the first time she came to study . . . by her-self." She looks up at the clock on the wall. "Closing soon." She disappears. I watch Autumn. Do not ask me why. She looks absolutely frustrated after a while.

Mrs. Carolyn does not have to ask Autumn to leave. Autumn stands up, knocking her book off the table. "Ahhhh!" she yells, before she looks around to see who might have heard.

I duck behind a shelf. She leaves the library, perhaps to use the girls' room. Passing by her desk, I see what she was trying to accomplish.

$$x = (64 \cdot 3) / 7$$

In secret, I scribble the answer on her paper.

CHAPTER 39

Autumn

S tupid.

I take that word out of the jar, ripping it up. Sitting on my window seat, looking out, I put in another one. *Intentional.*

I read it on a bus sign. BE INTENTIONAL, it said. WHEN YOU WANT TO SEND A MESSAGE, GIVE HER DIAMONDS.

I looked it up while I was at the library in school. It means on purpose, planned.

I been intentional about Adonis, wrestling, cooking, and being Peaches's best friend. Now I'm gonna be intentional about other stuff. That's what I'm hoping.

Downstairs my mom is cooking breakfast. She off today. Bacon. Cheese biscuits. Sausage. Walking downstairs, skipping the last step, I smell it all.

I squeeze the orange juice. Mix in a little cranberry juice and sugarless lemonade. Cutting up strawberries, I ask if she gonna drive me to school. "Gotta see Mr. E." Before she say anything, I ask about Malcolm X. "You ever read about him?" Online I read that he memorized all the words in the dictionary.

She seen the movie. I said I was gonna rent it but never did. Didn't read the book, either. If it wasn't so thick, maybe I would. "Let's rent it." She sits hot food on a tray. "This weekend, maybe . . . I don't know." Sitting next to me, talking about her job and school, she saying she's proud of me.

"Why?" I take two biscuits. It's nice eating anything you want.

Her hand stop mine, even while it's full. " 'Cause I can see you're thinking . . . figuring things out."

"Mom . . ."

"And you been going to class regular again . . . Running two and three times a week."

Intentional. I smile when that word come to my head. *Firstly, I'm being intentional,* I think. I wonder. Did Malcolm X use his words? Or did he just memorize 'em? Store 'em up in his head like boxes in a attic, not letting nobody know they was there? I wonder a lot of things lately. Not even sharing them with Peaches.

*   *   *

I walk into Mr. Epperson's room. It's just him there. His feet on the desk show how good the shoe shop fixes his heels. "Protein shake," he say, holding up a plastic container. "Now. My wife thinks I need to gain weight." Walking over to me, he ask how he can help me.

"Maybe it's too late . . . I don't know." I'm rubbing my hair. Grease gets on my fingers. I stare at them, wiping my hands on my pants.

He hand me a tissue. "Well . . . ?" He ask if I know why I'm here.

I know. But it's hard saying it. 'Cause I decided . . . once I say it . . . I gotta do it. Be intentional. Only I keep thinking math is so much work, a lot of reading. And reading and me equals . . . I don't say it. I promised myself I won't say things like that about me no more. Even if it's true. I won't say the words. I don't know. Maybe speaking 'em out loud (*stupid, illiterate, dumb*) turns 'em into something. Something we can't see, like poison gas, killing us. Killing me anyhow.

Standing tall and straight, holding my hands close to me, folded, I clear my throat. "Mr. Epperson!"

He salutes me. "Yes, Autumn."

"I need tutoring! Help 'cause . . ." My fingers cover my face, pick at my neck, pull my shirt down. "I'm good at stuff, Mr. Epperson. . . ." I don't want to cry. "But —" I'm not gonna, either.

Adonis knocking on the door. Mr. Epperson is rude to him when he say, "Not now."

Him seeing me cry would be the worst thing. Or hearing me say what I'm trying to say. I'm glad Mr. E. shuts the door. "Autumn." He clears his throat, too. "How can I help you?"

He gonna make me say it. "I don't know —" I'm turning around to leave, but he stops me.

"So you came to compete?" He take out his grade book. "Against this girl?" He show me all of my grades. "She's a fierce competitor. Gonna try to take you down. Make you think you can't do math . . . since she thought she couldn't do it." He coughs.

I read them to myself. Sixty-three. Sixty. Fifty-eight. Sixty-nine. Seventy. Sixty-one. There's even a forty-two and a half here.

Mr. E. is right. That girl who took these tests, she hate math — only wanted to put numbers on a page and sit the pencil down. "I been —"

I can't see it. Can't see ever getting better.

Breathing in deep. Exhaling. I get my words out quick so I can't take them back. "I been thinking . . . if I . . . when I . . ." I tell him I'm coming to tutoring three times a week. He ask about wrestling. Season's over now. Plus my parents say the same thing they did in January. I can't be on the team till something between me and reading improve. "No kid can help me, either . . . with math, I mean." That's my own rule that means Adonis is not welcomed. Peaches either.

That's fine with him, he say. Show up tomorrow for tutoring. "And be —"

"Intentional."

"— prepared. Books. Pencils. Calculator," he say.

"Intentional," I say to myself.

CHAPTER 40

ADONIS

She's practically skipping out of his room. Twirling a feather in her hand as if she were a three-year-old. Her dress, spinning colors, shows her thighs, strong and thick. I should not have stared.

Lately, she has this way of looking at me as if I didn't exist. She does not smile much at me, either. Holding her books high up to her chest like they're a shield, she keeps her distance. "Hello," I say.

She speeds up, walking past me as quickly as she can. Blocking students in the hallway, I sit staring. In the past, she would have said, see you later. Call me. Take me to the movies. Something.

"Hello, Adonis."

"Hello, Mr. Epperson. I need to speak to you about Patricia."

Standing, he waves his hands. "Can't. Not now. I have a staff meeting. I need tons of copies," he says, leafing through his desk papers.

"But —"

He apologizes. "Tomorrow I can talk."

I caught Patricia two weeks ago. Mr. Epperson has missed five school days since then. If I go to the principal, he wouldn't like it. If I don't speak up soon, well — integrity. Honor codes. They matter.

Autumn has not made it very far. She's standing beside her teacher, giving hugs to some guys from the team when they pass by. High on her toes like a ballerina, she's giggling about something Allen is saying to her. Slowly, I push myself up the ramp, thinking how silly she is.

The other evening, Ma and I were discussing Autumn's attributes. I thought it was a fruitless conversation at first. But later, I saw her point.

Autumn does not cheat. She speaks to everyone. Besides wrestling, smiling is her favorite activity. She will tell you everything about herself. Too much, I believe. Those are a few of the things I've written down. "She is a strong competitor, everyone likes her, and she thinks you are wonderful." Ma wanted me to add those.

The list is at home. Under my mattress. In an envelope. Taped closed.

Classes have not begun as of yet. I go to my favorite spot, the library.

Upstairs, I pick through books on the shelf. I want something light, not my usual heavy reading.

"Yo, Adonis." Jaxxon is at a table with a girl, talking on his cell. Papers and books are spread everywhere. "What's up?"

Usually when he is at the library, he is consumed with Autumn and her friends. He hardly ever speaks to me. Most guys don't. "Hello."

He is working on a PowerPoint presentation, plus a seven-page English paper, he tells me. That's a surprise. I didn't know regular classes did that sort of thing. "I'm stuck," he tells me.

I think about that word and Autumn. I wish him good luck.

"You ever read this book?" He holds it up, shaking it. "I know what you thinking ... I read ... better than Autumn."

That is what people would say if I went out with her.

I can hear the person on his cell talking. Jaxxon looks frustrated. He has two pages done. He's never used

PowerPoint. I wonder, *Why is he asking me?* "Did Autumn begin her paper?"

She is in his reading class, not his English class, he tells me. When I pass him, he looks at me like I am pond scum. "Why she like you anyway?"

Upstairs, sitting at the table alone, I look over at Raven. She is still with that eighth grader. They hold hands under the table while they study. A few other girls, sitting in furry blue chairs low to the ground, fool with one another's hair. There are not many people here. Almost everyone is with someone else. It's weird realizing that you are always alone.

CHAPTER 41

Autumn

*A*in't got too much time. So I say it. "Miss Baker, I *can* read better. I got a plan." Getting help, tutoring, is part of my plan, I tell her while kids walking outta class push past me.

Reading books — that's in my plan, too. While I'm talking to her, my head saying, *You can't read. Never will.*

Raising my voice, shouting like I'm trying to speak over somebody talking right next to me, I say, "I'm starting with the thin ones . . . at home . . . by myself . . . !" I ask her, "Do graphic novels count?"

Her arms stay folded. But her smile gets wider, listening. Stepping aside to let kids out, she say how proud she is of me. "Over the last few months, all I could think was . . . I'm losing another one of my babies." She standing back, looking at me like I'm on a runway, modeling.

"You walked in late so many times . . . missing half the period. The entire thing, some days." Shaking her head, letting out a deep breath, she telling me that teachers want students to excel. "When we all see you losing ground, baby, it's heartbreaking."

I'm embarrassed. Proud. Scared, too. It's hard saying out loud what I'm gonna do. 'Cause it mean she and Mr. E. — all my teachers — expecting me to do it. "What you think, Miss Baker?"

Her arms feel like a warm Snuggie, wrapping tight around me. My heart beating fast. Can I do it? Gotta do it. Read better. For me. *You gonna fail . . . like you always do,* I hear myself say, way deep down inside.

Wrestlers win first in their heads, Coach says. Readers, too, I figure, wondering sometimes if I ain't my own opponent.

Going up the hall, I see him, Adonis. Twice in one day. Plus I go to the library for lunch today. I'll see him there — won't chase him. But I still like to watch him out the corner of my eye anyhow. One day I won't like him. Today he making me twinkle inside, like a planet not discovered but still shining brighter than the moon.

"Hi." Dang it. Didn't mean to stop.

"Hello, Autumn."

I like when he has a fresh cut. They put good-smelling stuff on his hair. Even when he gone away from me, I smell it. *Keep walking, Autumn Knight*, I'm telling myself.

Sitting in his chair, squirming, he looking up at me. I look away. It's hard. But I do. Now my feet moving, taking me away from him.

Peaches grabbing me by the arm, pulling me off. "I need to speak to you."

She upset, talking low, looking back at him. He know, she say. And he gonna tell on her. "Mr. E. wants to see me." She stops. "Adonis will be there, too."

"Who?"

"Adonis."

"Adonis?"

She telling how when he came to class, he saw her cheating. She ain't tell me earlier.

"Pattie's gonna kill me." I hear her say under her breath. "He beat me. He's smarter than me."

Adonis is smarter than most everybody. I don't know if he smarter than her, really. "You just stuck" — I bend down, pointing to gum hard and dirty on the floor. Can't just pick it up or scrape it with your fingernail. You need a knife. Something strong — "stuck like this gum." Walking up the hall, my arm around her, I tell

Peaches Adonis is stuck, too. "I'm not talking about that chair." Looking at me, she smiling. "He stuck in here." I point to my head. "Scared, I think." I tell her to think about it. "A smart boy like that with no friends. Me cute. And he don't want me. Scared."

She laughing, saying he not afraid of nothing. "Even in the pond. He never screamed."

"You saw him?"

Peaches look like she just got caught cheating. "Yeah. I was there."

PINNED

In football, everyone wants to see a touchdown. In hockey, it's the puck fiercely flying past the goalie and into the net that makes the crowd cheer. In wrestling, it's the pin.

Sometimes at the end of a match I wonder, has anything in life ever pinned me? Held me down? Patricia would say yes. She would point to the pond incident as her proof. But I would disagree. I think about the incident a lot. I will for years to come, I believe.

But nothing will pin me down or stop me. Determination should be my middle name. Autumn is determined, too. Even when I think she's losing, she seems to come out ahead. Can anything pin her? I'm not certain anymore.

CHAPTER 42

ADONIS

A donis." When Autumn says my name, it sounds as if she's singing.

The period is almost over.

"Can I talk to you? In the back?"

Only volunteers and employees are permitted there. I explain this to her, while my wheels turn. "Just this once," I say.

Autumn sits in a chair beside me, leaning her elbow on a pile of books placed on the table. *Hush.* That's a good title for a book, she says. Then she brings up Patricia, and how sorry she is for cheating in math. "Please, Adonis. Don't tell. She won't do it no more."

I pull at the knot in my tie. "How many times did she do it, Autumn?"

She does not know the exact number, but Patricia has been cheating off and on for months, she says. She ruined the curve, I tell Autumn. Cheated on her friends, not just the test. "I have to tell."

I do not want her to see me upset. I am concentrating on books all around me. They are stacked on shelves, sitting in boxes. I work hard when I come to the library.

"You don't know her," she starts off.

"I don't know her?" I'm trying very hard not to upset myself. "You do not know what you are talking about, Autumn Knight." I am livid. She tells me that Patricia's parents pressure her to do well. "That's no reason to cheat."

"She just . . . thought . . . well."

Nothing infuriates me more than someone who thinks they know more than they do. "You cannot tell me anything about Patricia. I know my own cousin."

She hops out of the chair. "Cousin!" Picking up books like they're dirty dishes from a table, she walks around aimlessly. "Y'all cousins?" she says, sitting the books near the cabinet. Scratching. She has not done that for a while.

I take off my watch. "She's my father's oldest cousin's daughter. We never see that side of the family."

Patricia would never tell her. So I do. Listening to the story, she cannot believe her ears. "I would have drowned. But Macon called the police, and two other boys held my head above the water." Picking at the frayed band, I shove the watch in my pocket.

It's been a long time since I've told the story to anyone. I do not think I will tell it ever again. I still get e-mails from teachers who ask if I am doing well. They always mention the pond. I did not drown. My reputation as the boy who could do anything did.

When I am famous, they will still talk about it. When Autumn is an adult, people will forget about her poor grades. They will only remember that she was a great wrestler. The only girl wrestler on our team.

Tears well up in Autumn's eyes. All this time, she never knew the full story. It's worse than she thought, she tells me. "I just want you to know." Her finger slides down my nose. "You ain't deserve to be treated like that."

I lean forward. Finding her lips. Tasting cherry this time.

Pulling her into me, I open my eyes wide and stare. Kissing her again, I think of the day in the pond. And try not to cry.

CHAPTER 43

Autumn

*A*ll right. He's my cousin. So?"

Peaches doing me like Adonis did, trying to get away from me. Turning left at the end of the hall by the bench, she just about running past Mr. E.'s room. Doubling back. Speeding up. Like I ain't faster than her.

I block her. "I'm . . . your best friend. How . . . come I ain't . . . know?"

She got on flats. But they new. It's their first day on her feet. Catching her breath, picking at the loose skin on her heel, she say, "He's my cousin. Now you know. Quit asking me questions."

She taking the stairs, with me right beside her. Step after step, I ask her again, "How he your cousin? And y'all hate each other —"

"Leave me alone, Autumn!" She thinking he already told Mr. Epperson she a cheat. "That's Adonis. Squealer." Her other shoe come off when we get to the basement. We pass the weight room. I quit talking when we get near the wrestling room. Some of the guys are in there. "Hey, Autumn —" Zack telling me to hold up.

I keep it moving. Jogging past Peaches, pulling open the first door I get to, sitting beside the pool. I worry for my hair.

Sliding her feet in the water, Peaches making circles. "Part of our family lives on this side of Thirty-Seventh Avenue. Some live on the other side."

A bridge separates Thirty-Seventh Avenue once you get past town. On that side, houses got ceilings high as heaven, five or six bathrooms, tennis courts, and next-door neighbors who need a car to visit you. Where I live, we hear the people next door brushing in the morning. They got the malls over there. We got churches, Laundromats, and dollar stores.

Peaches telling me they got doctors in her family on the other side of the bridge. "Plus a professor, two lawyers, and a judge." She keeps at it, talking about some reporter on Channel 11 who is sorta kinda related to her daddy's side, too.

I wanna say she lying. I see in her eyes she's telling the truth. My family's just regular. My grandmother work in the lingerie section at Macy's, fitting bras and folding slips. My aunts work at Target and the nursing home on Eighth and Dickerson.

Peaches's toes come out the water. Holding her knees tight, she say, "Ever since I was born, they been telling me about that side. How I need to do like them. Be like them."

Her father hasn't spoken to that side since she was little 'cause of some fight he had with Adonis's father way back when. "I don't even know what it was about."

She never met Adonis's father. "He died before Adonis was eight. They say" — she put her feet back in — "he was too old to be a father. You know what I'm saying?" She looking at her legs. "If you wait too long, things can happen to the baby. That's what they say. My father was old. Sixty-five when I was born. We came out fine. There's five of us. My mother's his third wife."

The gym teacher come in, asking what we doing. "Out." She points to the door and picks up wet paper.

Heading out, my wet feet squishing in my shoes, I ask Peaches, "Do he live in a mansion?"

"Adonis?" Laughing, she say his mom moved to this side of the bridge, near the park, when he was in third grade. "They have a elevator." She was there once when they first moved in. Adonis's mother is a intensive care nurse, Peaches tells me.

I always wanted a doctor in my family.

"My father says they think they're better."

"What you think?"

"They tell me not to get outdone by that boy." I think about our third-quarter grades. I flunked math. She got her A. Seeing her face, I wonder if she think it was worth it.

Pulling off my shoes, drying my feet with my socks, I ask how long she been hating him. She start talking about last year. She was good at math till then. "All I said was . . ." She stop to clear her throat. *Adonis. I can't understand algebra, no matter how hard I study. Could you tutor me?* She breathing hard. "He was in algebra II," she says, "he could do my homework in his sleep."

Asking him was hard, she say. Her father woulda killed her if he knew. She had all As in everything else. Her teacher was hard to understand, even when she went for help. Miss Pattie and Peaches's father kept pushing her. Do better. Be better. So she went to Adonis.

"He said no?"

"He didn't say nothing."

"I know how that feels." I tell her about him and my

reading. I ask about the pond, the final exam. "Did Emily's brother give you one?"

"Good grades, straight As . . . in my family . . . are the most important thing . . ."

She holding on to my arm, admitting she went to the pond, saw everything.

"Why ain't you do something?"

She talking about seeing bubbles. How he went down in the water more than one time. "I couldn't . . . move. It was like, like my whole body was stone." She couldn't scream, either. "Just look. Like I was watching a movie. I prayed. I did that."

Some boys walked by and helped him. Her story is the same as Adonis's when she gets to that part. By the time Peaches got home, it was dark. Her shirt and pants was wet.

"What Miss Pattie say?"

She never told her mother what she saw. Miss Pattie read the story in the paper, transferred her here when she heard Adonis was coming. "It's a good school, if Adonis is here. That's what they think."

She looking up the hall, past me, saying her parents is right. "It's a good school."

"I —"

"I'm gonna live in Paris, Autumn. . . ." Our arms go over each other's shoulders. "And be famous and rich. I'll only come home for Thanksgiving."

"I like rich. But, Peaches" — I stand so we looking eye to eye — "don't cheat no more."

"Auddy?" It's Coach.

Ain't seen him for a while. I been ignoring his e-mails.

Peaches hugs me. "I'm scared," I say.

"Me, too."

"Talk to him." I look at her. She looks at me. We both said the same thing at once.

Coach waving me over. Peaches walking away. All my nervousness evaporating when I walk into the wrestling room.

CHAPTER 44

ADONIS

We have a code of conduct at our school. No cheating. Some of us take it seriously. I am in the honors society, which does not only mean I make high grades. It means I aspire to do the correct thing.

Autumn wants to know if I'll report my cousin. Mr. Epperson has not been able to meet with me. He's at school, thankfully. It has been difficult catching up with him. I'm not certain what I'd say now if I did. Moral dilemmas — we've studied them in class. Experiencing them firsthand is tough. I have been here before. I'm only fourteen. Why does this keep happening to me?

"Adonis." Autumn is handing out cupcakes. "For you." Soon we'll be taking state tests. She wanted to do something nice: freebies for as many people who would like them.

Her cupcakes have vanilla icing, sprinkled pink, with a fuchsia *P*, for Pinned, inscribed on the top. Mine is even more unique. I have a cupcake bearing my initials.

Autumn's feather matches the icing. April is breezy, so the feather's bent nearly in half. Rushing over to Jeff, she almost trips. I think her legs are my favorite part.

"*Free cupcakes.* That's how you say it, Jeff. You gotta be louder."

Jeff and a few of the van kids are volunteering today. Autumn offered to make them a special treat for Monday if they helped out.

"Three treats," Jeff shouts. Leaning on his crutches, he takes a cupcake from Tyreanna's tray and offers them to people passing by. The colored sprinkles sparkle in the sun.

I look at Autumn, amazed. She sees me smiling and asks if I'd like to hand them out, too. "No."

She sits a tray on my lap and walks away. Students — the regulars — walk past with their hands held out. They say my name when thanking me. I did not know they knew me.

Patricia comes late. Together she and Autumn hand out sixty-five cupcakes. They spent all weekend baking. That is the reason Autumn and I only spoke a few times. I was upset with myself for texting her thirty times on Saturday. Ma was amused. Another moral dilemma.

My cousin does not speak to me. She hardly looks at me. Autumn wants us each to apologize, to make up to each other. For once, Patricia and I are thinking exactly alike. We will never be friends.

Near the elevator, beside the old teachers' lounge, Autumn asks if she may kiss me. I notice that she says *may* sometimes.

We are a secret. No one is supposed to know. It was her idea for it to be this way. I think it's a good one.

"I love you." When she says that, you can tell she means it.

I love kissing her. I cannot explain what happens to me when our lips touch. I can't breathe. I need oxygen. I think differently, like Autumn is okay just the way she is.

Holding up a cupcake, she says we should eat it together. She peels back the yellow paper, splits the cupcake in half, and loops her arms through mine. We both take a bite. I am looking around because this is totally irresponsible — stupid, crazy Autumn stuff. Of course we kiss.

Walking toward the elevator, she brings up math. Tutoring is helping. Lots of things are still very difficult for her to understand.

"I can —"

"Nope." She presses the elevator button. "We got our deal."

She will leave me alone about Patricia. I will leave her alone about school, unless she asks for help.

Sighing, she asks if she is ever going to understand the stuff. We are on the elevator when Autumn inquires about Mr. Epperson. "You think . . . he gonna be okay?"

He just told us recently. He has cancer. Some people are afraid of the word, not me. He smoked for many years. When he went to his doctor to see if he was a good candidate for weight reduction surgery, they gave him an exam. "He'll be okay," I tell Autumn. But I'm not so sure.

Sitting on my lap, her head lying on my shoulder, she holds up my arm, checking the time.

"Your watch secret. I figured it out." Her index finger circles the cracked crystal.

I freeze.

She holds my hand close to her heart, seeing all that I've tried to hide. "It's rusted."

Mud. It will stop a watch. Your arms will get tired if you hold them up for long.

I am extraordinarily quiet for a while, uncertain. Autumn talks so much. What if she tells someone? It's my secret. My life. I have a right to privacy.

She takes both of my hands in hers and squeezes. I stare at the beige walls, and sigh. "My father said, *'This is my watch. Protect it. Pass it along to your children. When they hear it ticking, that will be my heart speaking.'*"

I keep my word. I never give it lightly. Patricia broke my word. We are family. Families honor and protect. She broke his heart.

"I have to go, Autumn."

She holds the watch up to her ear. "It doesn't tick," I say.

"You tick," she says, kissing me. "That's what I care about."

Elevators at this school move quickly. At times I wish they didn't.

CHAPTER 45

Autumn

*M*iss Baker sitting on my desk, her bare legs crossed. "I like what I see, baby."

I made all the tutoring sessions she and me had for a month and a half. I come before school, with sleep in my eyes, sometimes. It's hard. But I'm here.

"Look what can happen when people put their minds to it." She agreed not to make our class read out loud so much now. She said I helped her see it's not always the best thing you can do for a kid. "Ready?"

I'm holding my breath. "I think."

She goes to the front of the class. She'll time me for the next twenty minutes. It's just her and me at tutoring. I'm supposed to read this chapter and answer the questions once I'm done. Inside I feel like Jell-O. Cool and shaky. I been working on these two chapters for two weeks, even reading 'em at home and looking up words.

The other day I asked Peaches if she would help me sound out words I couldn't pronounce in a book I was reading on my own. She still talking to me. And cooking with me. But she different. I did not choose sides — I want 'em both in my life. Adonis ain't tell yet.

School's ending in a month. I'm hoping all her dreams come true: algebra II over the summer, honors geometry in the fall, me and her opening Pinned, all grown-up and happy.

"Go," Miss Baker saying.

As soon as I start, I'm stuck on the second question. Picking at my teeth, twisting the red plastic ring on my finger, I worry that maybe Miss Baker will give up on me one day 'cause she'll see that reading and me equals zero.

"Breathe," she say from the front of the room. "Otherwise you may get nervous and forget what you know, baby."

I breathe. She's right. You hold your breath even when you don't know you doing it. *Relax*, I tell myself. The answer to the next question come then. *Try*, I remind myself when I get stuck again. Why is it so hard for some people? I try not to ask myself that again.

Breathe. The next question got two parts. I look out the window. May is a pretty month. Not perfect. But getting better.

"Five more minutes."

It's not a long test. She say shorter work best for struggling readers. I erase only once. I think that means I know what I'm doing. I write and read and scratch. Looking at the clock, I speed up.

"Pencil down." She come to my desk, smiling. "You did well?"

"I don't know."

"I think . . . well . . . I should be quiet."

Taking the paper to her desk, she marking it right away. "Well . . . baby. Nice job."

I'm almost shaking. I mean, I really studied this time. Telling myself I can be a better reader. It's so hard. I'm starting to believe, though. I can get on grade level if I don't give up. "Miss Baker . . ."

She staring at my paper. "Yes, sweetie?"

"How many did I get wrong?"

When she done marking, I walk over to her and look down. "Seventy-five." It's written in big, red numbers. "That the first time . . . in this class."

"It's the beginning," she saying, "of you reading better and better."

Leaving her class, I go looking for him like the way he looked and found me the other day. At the library, I see him working. King of the books. That's a good name for him. That make me the queen.

Sneaking up behind him, covering up his eyes, I say, "Break time."

He looking around 'cause he still be worried about what people think.

It's almost empty in here. School's over soon. Mrs. Carolyn's in the back. He always gonna ask permission, do the right thing, be good. That's okay. It's him.

He hand me *The Autobiography of Malcolm X.*

I'm looking over the jacket. "Eyeglasses make you look smart." Turning to the back cover. Telling him about my test and how it went. He congratulating me. I'm congratulating myself, too. It wasn't easy. It been hard this whole year. Wrestling — I miss it.

He turning up the hall. I'm sitting on his lap, listening to him ask why I like to break all the rules. I point to the way we should go.

At the fountain by the bridge, drinking at the same time. Our lips ice-cold and warm. I think I hear him say, "I love you, Autumn Knight."

ACKNOWLEDGMENTS

Thanks and appreciation go to the following:

My editor, Andrea Davis Pinkney. You are the best. I could not have done it without you.

Coach Chris Edmonds (Pittsburgh Perry High School). Thanks for making yourself and your team available. Your insight and knowledge about wrestling were invaluable. Your kindness and warmth meant a great deal.

Yolanda Harris and Kathy Payne. Your wisdom and friendship over the years has comforted and strengthened me. And made me chuckle, too. Thanks for taking this journey with me.

Caribou Coffee (Freeport Road). I wrestled with this novel for many years. How helpful it was during the final 365 to find myself at your shop, windows pouring forth sunlight as readily as a warm cup of coffee from a pot. Friendly faces. A quiet space where silence does not enter, yet one's muse surely can and does. I had several breakthroughs there, proving that the right place and space does matter.

ABOUT THE AUTHOR

Sharon G. Flake exploded onto the literary scene with her novel *The Skin I'm In,* for which she was named a *Publishers Weekly* Flying Start. Since then she has become a multiple Coretta Scott King Book Award Author Honor winner and has been hailed as the voice of middle-grade youth and a Rising Star by the *Bulletin of the Center for Children's Books.* Many of Sharon's novels have received ALA Notable and Best Books for Young Adults citations from the American Library Association. Her writing has been applauded for its on-point narrative that explores issues affecting teens from all walks of life. She lives in Pittsburgh, Pennsylvania. Please visit Sharon at her website, www.sharongflake.com, and on Facebook and Twitter.

Be a part of
THE REVOLUTION OF EVELYN SERRANO

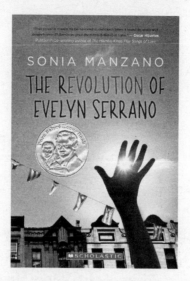

A Pura Belpré Honor Book
Winner of the Américas Award

★ "This wry, moving debut novel does a great job of blending the personal and the political . . . while the family drama and revelations continue right up to the end."
— *Booklist*, starred review

★ "Characters of surprising dimension round out the plot and add to the novel's cultural authenticity . . . A stunning debut."
— *Kirkus Reviews*, starred review

"An important story about activism, acceptance, and love. Sonia Manzano vividly portrays a neighborhood in turmoil, with embraceable characters who change history."
— Pam Muñoz Ryan, Pura Belpré Award-winning author of *The Dreamer* and *Esperanza Rising*

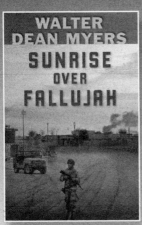

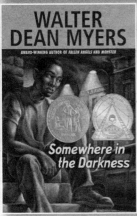

this is teen

Want to find more books, authors, and readers to connect with?

Interact with friends and favorite authors, participate in weekly author Q&As, check out event listings, try the book finder, and more!

**Join the new social experience at
www.facebook.com/thisisteen**